"A fascinating story written in superb language! It will not allow you to put down the book till it is finished. Having operated in counter-militancy operations along the Shamshabari Range and on either side of Pir Panjal Range in Jammu & Kashmir, I find the description of the terrain, locales and combat activities as authentic as can be. Only a Special Forces officer can go into such details."

—Gen VP Malik (Retd), Former Chief of Army Staff

"Another fascinating novel by Abhay Narayan Sapru, a third by him, that takes you through the challenges, tribulations, sweat, blood and gore of militancy and counter-insurgency in Kashmir. His characteristic inimitable style will keep you engrossed through to the last page of this narrative based on realities."

—Lt Gen Prakash Katoch (Retd)

THE SAVAGE HILLS

THE REAL SPECIAL FORCES STORY

THE SAVAGE HILLS

A Tale of Terror and Revenge in Kashmir

ABHAY NARAYAN SAPRU

First published 2021
Reprinted 2025

This is a work of fiction and creative liberty has been taken to describe people, events and places.

The map used in this book has been worked upon by the author, is not to scale and is for illustrative purposes only. No copyright infringement is intended.

ISBN 978-81-8328-549-0

Published by
Wisdom Tree
4779/23, Ansari Road
Darya Ganj, New Delhi-110002
Ph.: 011-23247966/67/68
wisdomtreebooks@gmail.com

Printed in India

My late parents, for introducing me to the joys of the written word.

The Special Forces, for all the experiences, without which the 'Harry series' wouldn't have seen the light of day. May you grow from strength to strength.

Ritz, for standing by in times good and bad.

Preface

The virtues of God are pardon and pity, they never were mine;
They have never been ours, in a kingdom stained with blood of our kin, Where the brothers embrace in the war-field and the reddest sword must win.

—Sir Alfred Comyn Lyall,
The Amir's Soliloquy

The print and the electronic media was full of stone-pelting in Kashmir. Burhan Wani, the poster boy of militancy, had been shot by the army. A fidayeen team had attacked an army camp in Uri and the latter, in retaliation, had carried out a cross-border surgical strike on so-called militant launch pads. The naysayers were predicting doomsday scenarios for the future of the valley, as I made my way up from Jammu on way to Bhadarwah town in Doda district. While the valley was on a boil, things had been rather quiet in the Pir Panjal mountains for some years now. I was visiting my old tramping grounds after over two decades. As I gazed across from Patnitop eastwards down the Chenab valley, the immensity of the landscape simply overwhelmed me. Wide valleys, hulking mountains and the Chenab, swollen and still because of the dam downstream, bisecting the land into a north–south divide.

The Pir Panjal mountains, especially in the Doda region, are huge unattractive mounds, shorn of tree coverage and cultivated in most places. No shapely summits etched against the skyline, no thickly-forested slopes. Where the mountain doesn't lend itself to cultivation on the heights, forests of Oak, Pine and Deodar add a brush of green. As far as the eye could see, mountain was stacked on mountain, dotted with tiny hamlets on a shoulder or a spur, their tin roofs shimmering in the distant haze. I was amazed at the expanse of the geographical canvas. The prodigious climbs we managed, burdened with back-breaking weight, and that too mostly at night.

The town of Bhadarwah or Nagon ki Bhoomi (the Land of Snakes) as it was called in the ancient times, had grown significantly from a quaint little place. I recalled how the place then was distinctly divided down the middle on religious demographics—with the upper half of the town referred to as 'Chota Pakistan' by the Rajput Hindu population. While Bhadarwah had been more of an interlude in my overall operational wanderings around the state, the intensity of soldiering, the vicious terrain and the experiences left an indelible mark which has not faded a shade over so many years. The thickly-forested ridge looked distant, with new settlements sprinkled further up on the ridge and the spurs, as I tried to trace along the crest line the exact spot where the incident perhaps had happened. I had been out seeking a contact with Manzur Ahmad and his gang of merry men, who had been sighted in some of the villages further down, when Murphy's Law ran me aground. By the time the guns fell silent, two civilians lay dead at my feet and another had been severely shot. My lead scout, a young paratrooper, received gunshot wounds. He was to die later in the military hospital at Udhampur. Needless to say, I came pretty close to meeting my maker that day. But then I guess my time hadn't come yet.

Doda district not being a disturbed area (it was never declared one), the laws of the land swung promptly into action and, in no time, an FIR had been lodged against me for multiple murders at the local cop station. Not to be outdone, the National Human Rights Commission (NHRC) also filed a case against me for human rights violation. The Army, feeling left out or perhaps under pressure, also now joined the fray and a field court of inquiry was initiated. Within days of coming back from the op, I was nicely wedged as they say, between a rock and a hard place, with the only saving grace that the militants hadn't yet taken a fatwa out in my name.

In the narrative, two of the main characters, Manzur Ahmad and RK, were real people and their story in itself merits a book. I did go out on ops with RK a few times, long before he became a menace to society. Anywhere else, the compelling account of their vendetta would have graced the silver screen; a gripping tale of death and mayhem, unleashed over remote hamlets, strung across a canvas of 25 square km of mountainous country, with all the other dramatist personae—the Army, police and the population—in their own way, sucked into a vortex of violence in their wake. But this was all happening outside the valley proper and was in too remote a corner of the state for any ripples to be caused in the media.

In the two-decade-long militancy in the state, security posts have been often fired upon and sometimes attacked, especially in the early stages of the insurgency. Who could have guessed things would only get worse and that they were a precursor to the fidayeen attacks that we are witnessing today. However, the incident of the militant attack on an Indian army post in Puneja village is described as I saw it and was perhaps the first and the only time an Army post was raided and overrun in the hinterland by a body of mujahideen.

The village of Puneja now extends right down to the road and I met up with Ram Kumar, the *nambardar*, headman of the village. When the post was raided, he had been away to Jammu and only came back once the fracas had died down. According to him, they had no warning of the impending raid and only late in the evening were they warned by the mujahideen to clear out of the village during the night. 'Lucky for you,' I told him, smiling and shaking his hand, for I was in a very unpleasant mood that fateful day. While Manzur Ahmad was still remembered by some of the old-timers, there were no current-day Robin Hoods to talk about. For the Army had completely eradicated militancy in the Doda and Kishtwar regions, with the last incident reported in 2011.

In 1994, an experimental commando Rashtriya Rifles or RR unit was raised for operations in Kashmir, on a 'son of the soil' concept. A majority of the men were locals from the state and came on deputation from the Dogra and the J&K Regiment, while the CO, along with a sprinkling of other ranks, were seconded from Special Forces (SF) and Parachute units. It was believed that the unit comprising Kashmiri Muslims and Hindu Dogras, specially trained and led by a nucleus of SF men would perform spectacularly, especially when unleashed on their own terrain. They would draw surrenders from their brethren, garner intelligence easily and present a fervour and motivation second to none, which comes when fighting for one's land.

The concept had been tested quite successfully by the Selous Scouts, an irregular Special Forces unit raised during the Rhodesian civil war. In the Indian context, the concept, while novel, was too simplistic in thought and hurriedly implemented, overlooking overarching nuances of selection, history and religion. Nevertheless, the performance of the unit was praiseworthy, notching up an impressive tally of kills in a short time. The local boys in the unit were often sent out on intelligence gathering and covert ops. The incident of Havildar Saifullah Khan mentioned in the novel has been narrated exactly the way it happened. For ease of understanding, I refer to the commando unit mentioned in the book by the more familiar nomenclature today as SF.

Like my other two novels, while a plot has been interwoven, the bulk of the narrative is based on true incidents and events. Al Faran's abduction of the foreigners from the Pahalgam valley was covered extensively by the media and details are freely available on the Internet. Sometime in October of 1995, when the crisis had been running for a couple of months, one team from our unit was heli-dropped into the Warwan valley to interdict any southward movement of the group, which was believed to be ensconced in a remote hamlet in the Warwan valley. With considerable international pressure building up on the Indian government to rescue the missing four foreigners, the fighting patrols from the team scoured the big mountains in an unabated drive to ensure the cordon remained effective. Al Faran, with their hostages, was to be ring-fenced and confined to their mountain fastness, till such time an op could be launched or a release negotiated. The efforts bore fruit in the killing of one and the capture of another Al Faran member.

The end game of the hostage fiasco was finally played out somewhere on the outskirts of Anantnag town resulting in the final annihilation of the remnants of the Al Faran group, along with their leader, Turki (The Turk). Considering the resources committed for the job and for all the hype and media attention the episode had garnered over the months, the perception would be of a well-coordinated operation—a culmination of months of toil, wherein the gamut of the state's law enforcement agencies, along with the Army, worked in tandem to bring about a meeting between the militant group and its executioners at the precise location and time.

But, strangely, reality is often at variance from perception and success in this case came about in the most undramatic fashion, quite familiar of course to those who have operated in insurgency environments, where luck plays as important a part as honest effort. A course mate of mine, Shukla, serving time with an RR unit, was out on an area domination patrol early in the morning. His sudden appearance in a narrow lane led to a hasty evacuation by a body of mujahideen who were waiting for a hard-earned cup of tea at the shop. Events would have unfolded differently had Shukla not noticed a dozen or so hot cups of tea on the table with no drinkers in sight. The shopkeeper promptly babbled the details.

The cat was out and this was Shukla's backyard. The group was cornered and the ensuing gun-battle raged through the day. By the evening, Shukla had lost two men, when a lone voice piped up from the opposition, requesting politely if they could borrow some ammo to continue with the fight. And I recall Shukla looking at me wistfully over his drink at the Anantnag transit camp and saying, 'You know I am a peace-loving man, brother, and under normal circumstances find it difficult to say no to a reasonable request, but the mother fuckers had crossed all limits. The account had to be squared.'

A reasonable man indeed was Shukla. Turki's body was later identified along with some of the other foreign fighters. The incident by then had run its course and the media had milked it for what it was worth, to merit a scant mention, as just another encounter in the strife-torn land of Kashmir. It is difficult for readers today to imagine the remoteness of some of the places mentioned in the book, especially the Warwan and the interiors of the Doda hills, for all-weather roads have now opened most of these inaccessible regions, including a road which goes over the Margan top.

While the book claims to be a work of fiction, it would be fair to say most of the events described did happen and I have tried to be faithful to the ground reality to the extent possible, without disturbing the plot. The novel attempts to capture the places, people and incidents, along with thoughts, motives and emotions of the myriad of characters that were thrown together in a maelstrom of life-changing events. Names, of course, have been changed in some cases for obvious reasons. Along the way, the book also attempts to convey a flavour of SF soldiering in a hostile and violent insurgency-ridden environment.

Abhay Narayan Sapru
Bombay

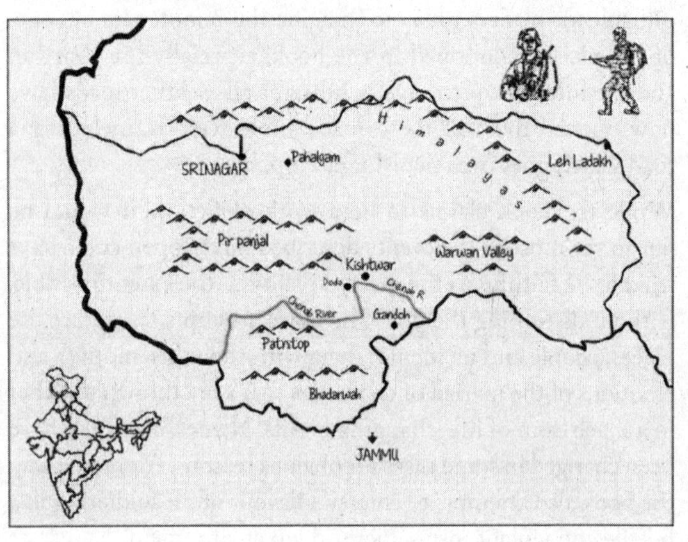

Himalayas
SRINAGAR
Pahalgam
Leh Ladakh
Pir panjal
Warwan Valley
Kishtwar
Doda
Chenab R
Chenab River
Gandoh
Patnitop
Bhadarwah
JAMMU

CHAPTER 1

Doda District, 1995

But this I know and find practically, that if you come to a dangerous place and turn back from it, though it may have been perfectly right and wise to do so, still your character has suffered some slight deterioration; you are to that extent weaker, more lifeless, more effeminate, more liable to passion and error in future; whereas if you go through with the danger, though it may have been apparently rash and foolish to encounter it, you come out of the encounter a stronger and a better man, fitter for every sort of work and trial and nothing but danger produces this effect.

—John Ruskin, Chamonix,1863

The lead scout suddenly stopped and went to ground. He ran a finger across his throat and pointed ahead. Harry dropped to his knees and looked in the direction. Through the thick Deodar forest, he saw the flickering orange flames of a fire about 100 metres ahead. The fire looked warm and inviting after the hard, wet night of climbing. The rain had ceased and it was just after first light. Under the canopy of the forest, the shadows of the night still lingered. A light breeze ran through the trees, rustling the undergrowth and picking up the flames, the crackle of the fire carrying across to the waiting men. As breeze rippled the forest canopy, it dislodged a thin shower of cold rain water on them. The air was crisp and carried the odour of damp earth and rotting vegetation.

For the SF troop, it had been the mother of all nights and had taken them nearly nine hours of hard climbing in a mountain squall to finally hit the ridge. It had been dark as sin and a nightmare for climbing, for the path was narrow, unused and had been washed away in places. Vainly they had struggled upwards, slipping, falling and sometimes hauling themselves on all fours, clutching shrubs and bramble, which often came loose. Behind them, in the wide black chasm of the Bhadarwah valley, lightning quivered and dashed about angrily.

A shiver now ran up Harry's spine as the sweat evaporated on his wet back, or maybe it was nervous excitement in anticipation of the action to come.

The lightened sky through the foliage looked clear and it promised to be a beautiful day, as if nature wanted to wipe out all traces of an ugly night. They were covered in gooey mud from head to toe and at some stage during the night, had to cover the mouth of their rifle barrel with condoms, to keep the mud and rain out as they scrambled up, slipping and falling cross country. A condom tied down with a rubber band made the best protection for weapons and loose ammo during rain or water crossing. The army clearly had more important things to think about than figuring out minor practical infantry issues.

Don't know, don't care, improvise or perish was the motto up the army chain, for there are supposed to be no impediments for the infantry. Harry recalled a saying: 'Condoms should be used for every conceivable occasion' or was it contraceptives? But clearly whoever came up with that saying couldn't have envisaged this occasion. Either way, what a waste of good condoms, he thought, as he peeled it off the barrel, like a lady her gloves, and gently released the safety catch. His mind probably was responding to the anxious excitement on the imminent contact.

Harry was attached to an Assam Regiment company post at Bhadarwah town to conduct independent operations with his troop of twenty men. Having left their camp sometime after dusk, they had started the climb from Gupt Ganga on the Niru river to the Border Security Force (BSF) post at Masarata. From here the dirt track then wound its way further up the mountain to end at the BSF company post at Jai. The rain had started soon after, and by the time they had hit the post at Masarata, they were drenched down to their underwear and Harry was ready to call it a day. The only cheer was the hot tea and the hurried dinner they had with the BSF guys. It was 9 o'clock at night and Harry was tempted to call off the operation as the rain had been incessant and the weather threatening to get worse.

Since morning, Harry had carried a sense of foreboding. Perhaps, he thought, the demanding climb and the forbidding miserable weather was making his thoughts turn dark, like everything around him. But having spent enough time in combat, he did not banish the thought as a figment of his overtaxed and fatigued mind. In fact, he reasoned, if his gut feel was right, then contact was imminent and either way, one has to take one's chances. Military operations can't be called off on an individual's gut instincts. Before stepping out of the post, he did, however, ask the troop if each of them was carrying sanitary napkins, a standard operating procedure in lieu of the field dressing pads they never had—a poor substitute, but fairly effective in plugging gunshot wounds. None was carrying it, or any sort of bandage or trauma medicine. Harry had then told the base radio operator to keep the Assam battalion's frequency handy, as he would certainly be calling for a chopper evacuation.

'What do you think?' he now asked the local guide who was shivering.

RK, the young guide, was an ex-BSF jawan and had been let out from the local jail by the Superintendent of Police (SP) of the area. He was behind bars for multiple murders, destruction of property and assault, to name some of the more impressive of his crimes. If there was a crime he hadn't committed, Harry got the impression, it was clearly for a want of opportunity. For RK was one of those irascible men who enjoyed cruelty for the sake of it. His offence list was long enough to fetch him a permanent residence in jail. Under normal circumstances, he wouldn't have been allowed bail and would have certainly been handcuffed and under armed escort before being permitted to move anywhere outside his cell. But here, in an insurgency environment, the man was apparently granted freedom as and when a job came up. He was the SP's hitman operating from behind the legal safety of the jail.

Necessity often makes strange bedfellows and in an insurgency situation, one invariably lands up in the company of the worst scum of society. For they are the ones who see an opportunity and have the courage to take risks. Harry had interacted in his time with murderers, smugglers and local underworld dons and some of them were very fine fellows, provided they knew who ran the show. He had been reluctant to hand over a weapon to RK as he didn't trust the man's shifty eyes. After all, what was stopping him from disappearing back into his backyard with the weapon, for he knew the terrain and this was his land. The SP, however, had taken full responsibility and assured Harry that RK was like a trained parrot who, once the cage was opened, would go right back in.

The intelligence had been provided by the SP and RK was the guide and the bait. The target was Manzur Ahmad, the local area commander of the HM (Hizb-ul-Mujahideen)—an ex-BSF deserter and RK's school mate, course mate in service and his neighbour in the village. There was a vendetta being played out between the two and all they had to do was to maintain surprise and lay an ambush around the village. The general presumption was that once word leaked out that RK was in the village, Manzur was definitely going to show up to square accounts. After all, the bloodletting score between them stood at one–love in favour of RK. On his last excursion outside the jail, RK had managed to kill one of Manzur's uncles. All this Harry had gathered partly from the SP, who was a little guarded about his star killer, and more from the garrulous RK during the climb.

'The SP sahib is a good man,' RK had told him, 'he provides the weapon and allows me out as and when I want, or when he wants a job done. Ideally, he prefers if I am back in the cell by morning.'

Harry didn't ask him what he meant by a 'job'. In the business of violence, specifics are never discussed. What happens in an op area remains in an op area. It did seem a Jekyll-and-Hyde sort of a scenario to Harry. The boyish looking young man slipping out from the cell in the dead of the night and turning into this cold-blooded murderer. Harry was to discover later RK's intense antipathy towards Manzur and Muslims in general. A feeling he shared with his mentor and protector, the SP.

'Sir,' he said now, in a hoarse tense whisper, a feverish glint noticeable in his eyes, 'mujahideen. We are over 6000 feet, in a forest, the nearest village is an hour away and in any case no villager would have spent a night out in this kind of weather.'

'Right,' Harry said turning to the JCO, 'the main body to stay here on the track. I am going ahead to investigate with the lead squad.'

God's been kind, perhaps it's payback for all the night's effort, thought Harry. The thick Deodar trees and the waist-high undergrowth aided concealment and within a few minutes of easy stalking, they had closed in to twenty feet of the fire. Three men were squatting around the fire, the flames lighting up their gaunt features. A couple of others were still asleep wrapped up in their *pattu* shawls. God had delivered his part, except the men, who were a trigger's breadth away from death, didn't look like militants.

They were civilians and woodcutters in all probability, judging by the tools of their trade lying around and the freshly felled logs scattered about. Slowly Harry's men emerged out of the shadows and walked in towards the fire covering the men with their weapons and shouting instructions to raise their hands and drop into a kneeling position. Harry leaned against a tree, closed his eyes and inhaled sharply, as his adrenalin-pumped body strove for normalcy. It was perhaps the tree that saved his life.

The next instant, loud gunfire shattered the early morning calm. The suddenness and the proximity of fire stupefied everyone, leaving them rooted to the spot. No amount of training can prepare one for unexpected gunfire at close quarters. Behavioural scientists observing the scene would have identified the reaction of the group as the sympathetic nervous system response, known more commonly in laymen's term as the fight-or-flight reflex. The infantry manuals taught you to dash down, take cover and return fire, on the assumption you have composed yourself to engage effectively in that time. The SF viewed CQB or close quarter battle drills differently and followed what was taught years ago to the Special Operations Executives during WW II, by the heavenly twins—Fairbairn and Sykes. If ambushed, go with your instinct and fire first. For by the time you find cover, provided one is available, and compose yourself, you might be dead. Regardless of where you shoot, the opponent is as vulnerable to the sound of gunfire as you are, or to a bullet whizzing past his ears and if nothing else, at least it will make the bastard pause, giving you vital seconds to survive and react.

Briefly for a few heartbeats, Harry experienced complete physical and mental paralysis, then the mind recovered in all clarity. With alacrity borne of hard combat experience, he knew immediately it was incoming AK fire, from across and clearly very close range. It must have lasted a few seconds, but it seemed an age before it stopped. Like always, the quietude after the gunfire was conspicuous, still and complete.

His heart was going berserk in the rib cage, making a ruckus as if desperate to escape its captivity. The breathing was deep and definite and Harry sensed immediately that the danger that existed at that place and time was over.

The first emotion was the joyous realisation of survival. He had gone through this state of feeling before. Coming out of a firefight unscathed and rejoicing at having survived it. Strangely, the mind had recovered faster than the body, which was still reluctant to respond to his command and remained motionless, cowering behind the tree. He recalled Churchill writing somewhere, that there was 'nothing more exhilarating than being shot at and not being hit'.

Leaning out a little from behind cover, Harry now loosened off a burst or two instinctively into the undergrowth across the clearing. Then he noticed his buddy Aziz lying on his back, blood dripping down his Adam's apple. Forget quotes, he berated himself for switching off, just because he thought the danger was past.

'Sahib,' whimpered Aziz, 'I am dead.'

'Aziz, you are not,' Harry shouted, wiping the blood, 'it's just a scratch. Get up and take position there.' He pointed to a fallen tree trunk, as mobility returned to his inert body.

His mind was in control and racing for answers as he rushed towards the group—how many? Where, how did they miss them?

The sight which greeted Harry took his breath away. Two of the locals were lying on the ground and even at a glance he knew they were stone dead. Both were shot in the head. One was lying with his face in the fire where a part of his brain had popped out and was roasting, while a thick stream of blood sizzled in the fire. The other guy was lying next to him, his head split open neatly from the nape of his neck to the centre, as if a surgeon had gone to work on him. Harry wondered for just the briefest of seconds, at what angle had the bullet hit to open his head and split the brain inside so perfectly in half. A third villager was lying on his back, still in shock clutching his thigh below which a pool of blood was slowly collecting.

An old man was squatting next to him, holding his head in his hands and rocking gently, as if shaking off a bad dream. He had an expression of complete disbelief writ on his face while his eyes, wide with horror, were riveted on his dead comrades. He was clearly unhurt. Surjit, the troop's lead scout, a young man of twenty, was sprawled on his back in a bush, his weapon lying to one side and a glazed stunned expression creeping into his eyes. He had been shot through the stomach and a second round had smashed the butt of his AK, ricocheting through his right elbow. Perfect grade-A carnage, thought Harry. Except for the logs crackling in the fire, the silence was deafening and the scene straight out of a B-grade horror movie.

The transition from tranquillity to shattering violence had left everybody numb. A few seconds back, Harry had been viewing a normal scene and the situation seemed well in control—a fire sighed and spat, while people sat around gazing into its depth, as people are wont to do. A lightened sky heralded the day to follow, while a gentle breeze blew away gradually the last signatures of the night. None could have predicted how quickly things would change and for some, forever. Harry knew it would be a futile wild goose chase, as the militants coming up from the opposite side had the surprise on him and having loosened off a burst, would have by now scattered downhill. Phantoms in the mist. The foreboding had been right, it had never left him and now strangely, he suddenly felt light. As if an invisible weight had been lifted off him. The worst was over. He cursed himself for not heeding to his inner voice.

This was not the way it was supposed to play out, God, Harry thought. Why me, what have I done to deserve this? How was the mess to be explained? Doda was not even a disturbed area. His pessimistic reverie was shortly interrupted by a loud agonising wail from the old man.

'*Yah*, Allah! *Fauj ne maar diya*. (Oh Allah! the Army has killed us),' he screamed and the words echoed in the damp forest.

Harry cast a helpless look and briefly wondered how had he ended up in this carnage, in a forest, up on a mountain, in the back of beyond of Jammu.

CHAPTER 2

Bhadarwah

Our air is pure, our lives purer and our women the prettiest of all. We live a hundred years, Jenab.

—An Old Bhadarwah Resident

The area drained by the Indus and its tributaries is generally what forms the western Himalayas. The western outlier of the Himalayan system is the Pir Panjal range, running approximately 200 miles southeast from the Kishanganga river in western Pakistan occupied Kashmir (POK) to the upper Beas river in north-western Himachal Pradesh, with an average elevation of 13,000 feet. While anywhere else in the world they would have been considered a fine collection of mountains, here, lying in the shadows of the greater Himalayas, they seem rather unimpressive in comparison. The higher reaches are generally thickly wooded and Harry was often surprised, on reaching the top of a high mountain, to discover a rolling green pasture big enough to accommodate a nine-hole golf course.

A sizeable population of Gujjars inhabits the heights in summers, leading a migratory life with their flock of sheep and cattle and shuttling during the seasons between the hills and the plains of Jammu and Punjab.

From the Pir Panjals to the old region of Turkestan, except for the main valley of Kashmir and a few smaller valleys, it is only a stack of mountainous terrain. Harry had read about the region and knew that as an area of exploration it was probably the smallest when compared to the Poles or Africa but took an equal amount of time and effort to discover. As a yardstick of how important the region was for explorers, the Royal Geographical society from the time of its founding in 1831 till the end of the century had awarded twelve gold medals to various individuals—an inordinately large number of medals to be dished out, considering the size of the area explored.

However, the man who really contributed in the opening of the Pir Panjal belt was Godfrey Thomas Vigne. Relegated to the shadows of the more famous explorers like Moorcroft, Wolff or Jacquemont, Vigne was more a traveller than an explorer and crossed the Pir Panjals five times. He was, in fact, the first foreigner to visit the towns of Kishtwar and Bhadarwah. Harry wondered about the route he may have taken. Perhaps he came up from Jammu along the only road that connected the place now.

He looked down at the prone figure of Surjit on the stretcher and impatiently checked his watch. Why was the medical evacuation chopper taking so much time? After all, the Army Aviation squadron based at Udhampur was barely ten minutes away in terms of flying time and the weather was a pilot's dream. He thought about the past few hours following the contact.

They had patched up Surjit as best as they could with some cloth torn from his own turban. Harry had then turned to the old villager still in shock and offered him an air evacuation, if he could get his wounded man down to the roadhead.

'Get the villagers to help you,' he told the man, 'for I can't spare a single person. Other than carrying my injured man, I have to take all precautions I don't end up walking into another ambush. The bastards know I am hurt.'

Harry had instructed RK to lead and take the shortest path down to the roadhead. Time was of essence as Surjit needed immediate medical attention. They had descended through rough terrain for some time before emerging onto a beaten path. They then went through the village, the houses scattered and shut and all wearing a deserted look. Clearly the firing had driven the locals indoors. The column had suddenly come to a halt and Harry, walking in the middle with Surjit, had moved ahead to see what the problem was. He found RK deep in conversation with a pretty young woman who was spreading some laundry on a timber palisade. With one foot cocked up on the beam and chewing on a twig, a nonchalant RK seemed engrossed in an animated chat with her. Harry had lost his cool at the man and roughly shoved him back on the path.

'Get going,' he said angrily, 'a man needs medical attention and you are more interested in chasing the village skirts. If he dies on me, promise I will kill you!'

The girl had given Harry a sullen look, before disappearing back into the house. Probably feeling a little miffed at being insulted in front of the woman, RK carried on in a sulky mood. A little later, he had sidled up to Harry on the track and asked permission to stay back in the village. He was prepared to return the weapon if that worried Harry, promising to return to barracks or, in his case, a cell, within twenty-four hours with the latest intelligence on Manzur.

'What a stupid idea!' Harry had retorted. 'Don't give me this cock-and-bull story about gathering intel for me. Be honest—you have the hots for that girl.

'Understand clearly, I really don't care if you get killed, but right now you have been borrowed from the SP sahib. Once I hand you over to him, you are free to go wherever you want. By the way, I am well aware of your wild reputation. Any murder, rape or wanton vandalism will not be allowed on my watch. So, till then, fall in line. And incidentally, who is the chick?'

'That Sir, was Manzur Ahmad's house,' RK had answered gravely, 'and the girl, well, she is his stepsister. Manzur's father, you see, married twice. The girl is from his first Hindu wife. You give me some time with her and I will get you all the information you need on the man.'

'No way,' Harry had told him, 'no bloody way. All I need is a rape charge now, on top of a homicide case that is probably already on the cards. Is that why you got us this way, RK? Wanted a quick swipe at Manzur's family now that you were here with the guns backing you? And by the way, aren't you interested in meeting your own family?'

'Sir, the few who are left,' RK had answered poignantly, 'have already relocated either to Kishtwar or are now down in Jammu. My land lies fallow and my late father's house is in ruins.'

The trip down the narrow track, slushy with the night's downpour, had been a nightmare with soldiers taking turns at lugging Surjit on their back. It was a rough ride for him, with constant halts and change of backs, for Harry could see Surjit was in excruciating pain and drifting in and out of consciousness. Harry had walked alongside him uttering encouragement and prodding him from time to time to stay awake. Hitting the road, they had commandeered the first civilian truck on its way to Bhadarwah and taken it straight to the school playing field which was used as an improvised helipad.

The throb of the distant machine grew louder, breaking Harry's thoughts, as the metal bird landed in a cloud of dust. Eager hands slid the stretcher in. Harry squeezed Surjit's hand and told him to stay strong, promising a trip to the hospital soon to see him. Within minutes the chopper was airborne and following the road as a landmark, it rapidly disappeared out of the valley.

As the sound of the chopper faded, Harry's thoughts turned to the situation and how best to handle it—the gamut of things to be done. A sit rep to Battalion HQ reporting the incident, debriefing of the boys and most important, managing the Army higher formation and the local police which would now be baying for his blood for civilian deaths in an undisturbed area.

CHAPTER 3

Bhadarwah

For death was a difficult trade and the sword was a broker of doom.

—James Elroy Flecker, *War Song of the Saracens*

Manzur Ahmad was a short man, no different from most of his race, but to the beholder, his lithe 5-feet 6-inch frame gave the impression of lasting endurance and abounding energy. A childhood spent wrestling had given him a body that would have been the toast of a gym in any city. The sport and the hard outdoor mountain life had moulded muscles that people in urban environments often spend years trying to get in state-of-the-art gyms with personal trainers and all sorts of dietary supplements. And yet they would never have what this man had inherited because of his tough upbringing—a natural strength of body and mind. At eighteen years of age, he had joined the BSF and the disciplined existence with regular physical training further enhanced the inherent strength that he possessed.

He looked rugged, with a wrestler's broken cauliflower ears sticking out of his long hair. Half his face was covered under a thick beard, which as per regulations of his religious order, hung a fist's length below his chin and was quite disproportionate to his round countenance, making him look squat. The beard was one of the symbols of his chosen path of fundamental Islam. However, Manzur's rough peasant looks and demeanour belied a wily and cautious intellect that was always ticking and thinking ahead. At twenty-six, he was in the prime of his youth and had lived an eventful life. If militancy was slowly turning life hell for the population, for Manzur Ahmad it had been one hell of a militancy so far.

While the Army and the police were omnipresent in the valleys and towns, the mountains were bereft of their presence. As Doda district was not declared a disturbed area, the security forces were restrained in their approach to curb militancy and the local police, fearing for their families up in the villages, were rendered impotent and their absence quite conspicuous in the hills. The size of the mountains also helped—the climbs were prodigious, with numerous isolated hamlets scattered across yawning valleys and distant mountain tops, providing food and shelter out of choice or fear to the gun-wielding desperadoes. The rivers were raging torrents most of the year, with few crossing points. From the roadhead, it could take anywhere from ten to fifteen hours of climbing at night to reach some of the higher villages. Enough time for the jungle drums to spread the word about any approaching army column.

A mixed population of Muslims and Hindu Rajputs comprised the demographics of the area. The higher reaches in summer were inhabited by the migratory Muslim Gujjar community with their cattle and livestock. The heightened militancy levels in the Kashmir valley and the porous border with Pakistan also took the spotlight away from the area, with the focus of the Army and the government inclined more towards the annihilation of militancy in the valley and to the plugging of cross-border infiltration. The flotsam of unemployed mujahideen, drifting around in the aftermath of the jehad in Afghanistan, were promptly diverted eastwards by the Pakis and there was an influx of foreign fighters into Kashmir. While the bulk hung around in the Kashmir valley, a sprinkling of these seasoned veterans made their way to Doda and its environs, to bolster the nascent militancy. If a piece of real estate was designed for nurturing guerrilla warfare and insurgency, Doda district got a tick in all the boxes. Barring the towns, Manzur's writ ran across an area of approximately thirty odd square km of mountainous country, from Pul Doda in the north to Bhalla in the south and from Patnitop to Gundoh in the east.

These were early days of militancy in the hills and the ancient close ties that existed between the two communities were yet to reach the breaking strain imposed upon them by the resurgent religious divide happening in the valley. As long as Manzur left the Hindu population to their own devices, didn't harass or hurt them, intelligence wasn't forthcoming easily. Because of the distances and the terrain constraints, the odd piece of actionable intelligence was invariably stale by the time it reached the security forces and the delayed reaction time further diminished any chances of nabbing or killing the culprits. Given the circumstances, Manzur Ahmad and company were on a roll and if one stayed on the heights and didn't take unnecessary risks, the chances of meeting your maker were quite low.

Manzur had been holed up in a small distant valley, comprising the twin hamlets of Jora Kalan and Jora Khurd. Surrounded by thick fir forests and mountain ranges for miles, the location was ideally saddled midway between the towns of Bhadarwah and Gundoh and had become his de facto op HQ of sorts. Other than of course the remoteness of the place, Manzur had more personal reasons to be hanging around in the village, for he was besotted by a young married girl. For months now he had been trying to woo the young lady but to no avail. She seemed impervious to his charms.

He then switched tactics and had been trying to pressurise the husband to divorce her, so that he could tie the knot with her at the earliest. So far he had been very patient and wanted the matter wrapped up amicably, for he didn't want to antagonise the villagers. In his line of work, his longevity after all depended considerably on their support. However, he had made up his mind that if friendly overtures didn't work with the husband soon, the gun would be the final arbitrator to ease the decision in his favour. But that was to be the last resort.

In the meanwhile, a message had come from Malik for a meeting with him. Malik was a senior Paki mujahid from the Harkat *tanzim*, who had been quite active north of the Chenab in the Banihal belt. He had led a few good strikes against the security forces and, in the last op, the group had ambushed a CRPF convoy. They had simply engaged from the safety of the heights and opened up with all their weapons. The first volley had got them half a dozen kills, but the rest of the soldiers had managed to take cover. The local militants were jubilant with the success, but for a seasoned fighter like Malik, it was waste of an opportunity which was a godsend.

He had fought the Soviets in Afghanistan and was on his second stint for the so-called Jehad-e-Kashmir, having previously spent a year in the Lolab valley in north Kashmir. Ideally, he thought, if he had the right fighting men—the kind he had the privilege of fighting along in Afghanistan—under a withering fire from the cliffs, he would have closed on the target with just a few men and laid waste the vehicles. There were four buses packed with easily two hundred men, as juicy a target as it can get and what had they achieved? Absolutely nothing.

However, he was grateful for Allah's small mercies. They had got the few kafirs without buying any casualties on their side. This was lucky for he had seen how easily death could demoralise the local cadres. While all the foreign militants were mostly volunteers and had come of their own volition for jehad—to embrace death as their final goal—the local militants had a very different set of reasons. The proximity of their kith and kin made them less susceptible to taking undue risks. Most had got into militancy not for any theological religiosity, but for the free easy life it offered. While Manzur and his ilk had loose group affiliations, they adhered more to an undefined sacrament of the mafia code. Religion was a justification, weak governance an opportunity and unemployment the cause. Like most insurgency movements, it boiled down to politics of economics, for it had always been a hardscrabble existence up in the hills.

Malik's audacious hit-and-run tactics had made the security forces wary, prohibiting easy movement of convoys and forcing them to commit a lot of troops for road-opening duties. This meant trouble as the road-opening troops themselves now became easy targets. From the perspective of the Paki planners, while things had heated up for the Indians in the valley, bulk of the Doda belt remained relatively calm and it seemed the local militants were hesitant to engage with the security forces. Perhaps the leadership was weak, thought Malik. Instructions had come from higher-ups in the *tanzim* to torch the hills.

'The tinder is dry—a favourable wind blows towards the Pir Panjal—only a spark is needed. Escalate the conflict,' Malik was told, 'even if it means indiscriminate killing of the minority Hindu population. Set the Pir Panjal on fire.'

He sent a message to Manzur for a meeting, which was fixed for the next day in the village of Chakrabati. Manzur had picked the village as the venue, for it happened to be his home and would give him a chance to catch up with family, other than an opportunity to attend to a long-pending feud.

It was a five-hour walk to his village and Manzur left while it was still dark, with daybreak an hour or so away. It was always safer to travel before dawn as the Army generally preferred to operate during the day. The weather was atrocious and it had been raining incessantly. The path under the canopy of the forest gave some protection from the rain but it was dark as hell, and Manzur had to switch on his torch from time to time to ensure he hadn't drifted away from the main path. The rain beat a steady pattering drumbeat on his plastic poncho, as forked lightning sliced the dark skies, accompanied with thunder that ominously rolled across the black swathe of the firmament like a moving barrage. It was like a giant light and sound show with 3D effect, the flash of lightning intermittently illuminating the forest in a surreal ghastly white glow.

To the four locals this was not unusual weather, for it was the season of rain and the mountains often experienced these storms.

This one was a shade worse. But it was certainly terrible weather to be outdoors, thought Manzur. At the moment he was more worried about being scorched by lightning than by any Army patrol. They wouldn't dream to be out on a night like this.

'Turn your barrels down,' he instructed the others behind him. 'Remember the *masterji,* last year. What was his name...Ram Singh, I think. The idiot was walking in this kind of weather with his umbrella out, when the metal tip caught a nasty flash of lightning. I carried his body the next day for funeral in a state his wife couldn't recognise him. Scorched black, skin like parchment and curled up like a foetus. And imagine he was a teacher and didn't know metal becomes a conductor during lightning.'

'Everybody knows that, especially in the hills,' answered Aslam from behind with a sardonic chuckle. 'Perhaps he didn't expect it would strike under the cover of the forest. Good man, he taught me in school.

'When I was serving in the BSF,' continued Manzur, for he was in a chatty mood in spite of the inclement weather. After all he was a man in love. 'We were taught to cover all metal parts during such weather. In fact, we invariably lost men to such storms on the border, especially the guys in the communication bunkers, with their tall radio antennas sticking out like aroused dicks in loose pyjamas and attracting all the lightning from the heavens, like my beloved Razia does men, from the villages around.'

'And has the antenna effect too on them, Manzur Bhai,' retorted Aslam again, laughing. He was an old school mate of Manzur's and could take such liberties with him.

'Not a word about your Bhabi, sister fuckers,' cut in Manzur sharply, nipping in the bud any further talk about his woman and curtailing the ripple of laughter threatening to escalate into loud guffaws any moment.

'After we finish the meeting,' continued Aslam, diverting the conversation for he knew Razia was a sensitive point with Manzur, 'are we paying a visit to your dear friend RK's house?'

'Well, he is your classmate too, brother. Sure, etiquette demands we say hello to an old friend,' replied Manzur, 'standard operating procedures, whenever we visit the village. I still need to deal with his uncle after what he did to mine on one of his last trips home, provided the bastard is still hanging around in the village.' Manzur clenched his teeth in anger as he thought of RK.

He fell silent as his mind drifted to the days when they were children, growing up together and practically living in each other's home. They were neighbours in the village of Chakrabati, a small village at about seven thousand feet, lying just below a forested ridge line and comprising a hundred mixed Hindu and Muslim families. Most men worked their small patch of land producing maize, potatoes, beans and an inferior quality of apples and walnuts. A few of the families had men working in the police and in government offices in Bhadarwah town. The Muslims, converts from the same Hindu Rajput stock, had lived in peace with each other for centuries. And now the devil's wind had shaken the foundation, disrupting the balance of a hitherto tranquil life.

How times have changed, he mused. Both RK and he would hang around after school with a few other boys, spending time climbing hills, stealing apples and going down to Bhadarwah town for the odd trip to the market. They were classmates in school, the best of buddies and often took part in the local inter-village wrestling matches. They fought in the same weight category and Manzur smiled at the thought that he always got the better of RK in the pit. When they turned eighteen, both decided to join the army. But that year there was no army recruitment drive in Srinagar and by the time one was held in Jammu, neither could make it because of some domestic responsibility or the other. So they settled for the BSF and joined it together. Coincidentally they were slotted in the same company and platoon during training.

Their friendship only grew stronger and they were inseparable, addressing each other as brother and sticking together during training and rest. While Manzur continued with his wrestling, taking part in company competitions, RK who was more delicately built was the better runner and won all the cross-country events. But both the young men from the mountains impressed the instructors with their strength, fitness and an eagerness to excel. They were noticeably stronger than most of their other course mates hailing from the dusty plains of India. A healthy rivalry existed between the two friends, as they competed for everything, from physicals to academics. Their training officer looked at them with satisfaction and summed up their personal dossier with three attributes—hardy, cheerful and excellent soldier material.

Then their paths diverged as they were sent into different battalions. Manzur's battalion was deployed on the Pakistan border in Jammu sector, while RK's was on the Bangladesh border. The next time they were thrown together professionally was when both of them turned up for the commando course with the Army. A few vacancies were allotted to the navy and some of the paramilitary units. Being a prestigious course, only the best officers and men, mostly from the BSF and the ITBP (Indo-Tibetan Border Police), got a chance to attend the thirty-day hell on earth the Army had designed at Belgaum.

Both the hill boys excelled in the physically demanding tests and were the only students from all the outsiders attending the course, who could match up with the men from the Army. The two of them landed up with an Instructor grading. Going by their annual reports and course results, both the friends were high profile and their careers in the BSF seemed bright, with suggestions from higher quarters that they should appear for their officer's commission in the organisation.

But Allah willed otherwise, Manzur thought wistfully. The winds of change had been blowing steadily for some time north of the Pir Panjals in the valley and gaining momentum. The elders in the community were talking about supporting their Muslim brethren in the Kashmir valley and quite a few youngsters had crossed the border into Pakistan to receive basic training in arms and explosives, coming back with a weapon to flaunt their new-found power in the villages. Some of them often dropped in at Manzur's house and berated his father for allowing the son to serve in the infidels' army. Every time he came home on leave, his father and uncles would sit him down and lecture him on his duties as a Muslim. His *raison d'etre* for serving the nation was now under enormous pressure and he was finding it very difficult to defend his actions in the BSF.

'What,' they said, 'if your unit was posted here for counter-insurgency duties, would you be happy shooting one of your kith and kin?' So on and so forth went their arguments, sometimes gentle, sometimes cajoling, but often insinuating threats of ostracism from the community. Put under such incessant social pressure, any man would have cracked and it was just a matter of time before a spark veered his course from a proud law-abiding soldier to a mujahideen in Allah's army.

And the spark came from none other than his close friend RK, recalled Manzur. If it hadn't been for him, perhaps he would still have been serving in the BSF. On one of his trips home on leave, RK had gone across to pay his respects to Manzur's parents. He found the father reserved and not his usual jovial self. The uncle working in the fields joined him a little later and the two older men pitched into RK about the racial inequity and the need either for an independent country or to be a part of Muslim Pakistan. RK initially tried to discuss and then, out of respect, let them steam out their imagined grievances against the state and the majority Hindu population in the country. The situation rapidly spiralled out of control and heated words were exchanged, with RK finally losing control, especially when Manzur's father suggested that he should convert to Islam. Blows were exchanged and RK ended up giving the father a swollen eye. He had to make a hasty retreat, as the uncle turned up with a butcher's carving knife.

The letter bearing the ill-tidings of the incident caught up with Manzur, as he sat cleaning his light machine gun (LMG) after a night-firing exercise somewhere in the Samba sector close to Jammu. The contents of the letter, exaggerated to the extreme, had the desired effect on the reader, as it was intended to. Manzur read it slowly, ruminating over the contents and by the time he had gone over the letter a third time, his mind had been made up on the future course of action. The breaking strain had been crossed. Instead of depositing the weapon in the armoury, he dismantled the various parts, and shoving them in a kitbag, went back to his quarters in the main barrack. Spending just enough time to collect his money and change into mufti, he jumped over the compound wall behind and darted into the darkness on his way to the bus stand. Manzur knew once he hit the mountains, he would be safe like a baby in its mother's arms. For all it mattered, they could send the entire BSF in search of him and the mountains would swallow the lot.

The first thing he did on reaching home was to send for his friend Aslam. He then assembled the weapon and decided to pay RK's father a visit. His sister tried to stop him, mumbling something about the old man needling RK who had been rather restrained till the very end. Manzur snapped at her for taking sides with a man who had insulted their father.

'That's your Hindu blood talking, sister,' he shouted. 'Don't make me open my mouth any further, for I know where your loyalties lie. Now get out of my way.'

Manzur was beyond listening in his rage and roughly shoving his sister aside, strode out with his friend Aslam in tow, who had already joined militancy and was a member of the Hizb-ul-Mujahideen group. His intention was to basically give RK's father a sound thrashing and square up the account. Manzur had practically grown up in front of the man he was planning to rough up, someone he addressed as uncle. While he had been all worked up after reading the letter, now when the time came to act, he was assailed by self-doubt. As they hurriedly walked down the path, Aslam could see his friend's resolve weakening as he struggled with emotions. He promptly reminded Manzur how RK had no misgivings about beating up his father.

The loud knocking on the door was answered by the old father, wearing a surprised expression. One look at the familiar face and Manzur knew it was going to be difficult. Without giving the man a chance to say anything, he roughly pushed him back and stepped inside. That's when the old man made a mistake that would cost him more than a regret. Instinctively reaching out, he made for the wall on which hung a scythe. Perhaps RK had warned him about reprisal, or perhaps Manzur's weapon and threatening behaviour alarmed him, one would never know, but it gave Manzur the excuse he was waiting for. The wooden butt of the LMG, while designed to absorb the recoil of the weapon, is also a highly effective weapon for clubbing, especially in the hands of an angry young man trained for violence. Good soldiers are trained in bayonet fighting, to parry the adversary's thrust and strike edgeways with the stock to the face in one swift motion, before running the man through with the blade. But in this case, there was no strike, no countermove necessitated and no adversary.

Good soldiers in rage can also forget drills, especially if there is no bayonet fixed to the weapon and no armed enemy to confront. The butt of a heavy weapon is a brutal way to express pent-up emotion and Manzur set about it like a man gone berserk with a baseball bat. By the time Aslam pulled him away, with RK's mother screaming in the background, the man writhing on the ground couldn't have been recognised by RK as his father. His face was smashed to pulp, as if a road roller had gone over it and the broken nose laboured to draw in breath—breath which was getting scarcer by the minute. By the time, the neighbours collected and worked out the modality of carrying him down to Bhadarwah for treatment, the man had drawn his last breath.

Manzur Ahmad recalled the incident with a pang of regret. The retaliation from his side had been way above than was merited. He knew he had lost control. In his mind he tried to justify the killing in the name of jehad, but knew it was nothing short of murder. It was purely a personal honour kill and had nothing to do with religion. As he expected, it had not gone down well with RK and within a month the score was being settled. The body of Manzur's father was discovered by some village kids in a nullah with multiple stab wounds. While he had gone out to herd the cattle for the night, someone had dragged him into the nullah barely a hundred yards from the house and killed him.

What was worse, the killer had slashed the face with a knife rendering it unrecognisable. The disfiguring of the face was a message and Manzur knew very well who had sent it and what it purported. An eye for an eye, blood for blood and a father for a father. He only hoped, for the sake of his poor father, that the cutting up of the face was done as an afterthought, long after his father was already dead. Once the gloves were off, there had been no let-up in the killings thereafter on both sides. After the first murders, the disciplined law-abiding soldiers gave vent to their base instincts. There would be no more squeamishness about killing hereon and violent deaths of uncles, cousins and friends had followed.

What surprised Manzur while thinking over the events of the past two years was how RK managed to retaliate so quickly, for he knew the man had been dismissed from service and was already behind bars on charges of multiple murders. Clearly the SP sahib was hand in glove with RK, giving him the latest information and allowing him the freedom, as and when a killing was to be done. The strange thing was that no one had seen RK in the villages around. The clever bastard operated at night and was perhaps back in the safe confines of the jail by daybreak. Well, thought Manzur, chewing on a piece of Kalari, the dry cottage cheese he carried as an emergency ration, one of these days, he ought to ambush the SP sahib and figure out how to get RK killed in his cell.

The fact that he was a trained soldier, a deserter from service with a LMG and had killed a man in cold blood, got him immediate entry into the ranks of the Hizb-ul-Mujahideen. Much to the chagrin of the older members in the *tanzim* he was nominated as the commander of the Bhadarwah belt, an area loosely running south of the Chenab river from Gundoh in the east to Patnitop in the west. So far it had been a great phase and command had come quite easy to him. The ex-rising star of the BSF was now the man to watch in the hierarchy of the Hizb-ul-Mujahideen group.

Manzur now wondered why he had been summoned by Malik for this important s*alah mashwara,* discussion, at such a short notice. While he had never met the man, they had spoken on the radio from time to time. In spite of the fact that Malik held no official rank in the party, being a Pakistani, he still carried a lot of weight, especially when it came to decisions concerning distribution of weapons, money and other operational matters. His word had to be obeyed, for one wrong whisper from him to the handlers across the border and the tap would get turned off.

Daylight was breaking and a clear sky was visible overhead through the open patches in the forest canopy. Under the trees the nooks and corners were still dark. The rain had ceased and a light breeze murmured through the damp forest.

Aslam in the lead suddenly stopped and raised his hand. Manzur sidled up to him.

'What's the problem?' he asked in a whisper, 'We are nearly home. I can already smell my mother's food.'

'Someone's ahead,' replied Aslam nervously, 'I can hear voices in the wind and smell fire. There, can you see the smoke?' And he pointed straight ahead at the ridge line running perpendicular to them.

'Can't be the Army,' said Manzur, crouching down, as the others joined in for the discussion. 'They don't leave their posts in Bhadarwah and definitely not in this weather.'

'I have a bad feeling,' chipped in Aslam, who was a cautious man, 'let's turn back.'

'Haven't changed much since school, have you?' Manzur said, smiling. 'Still the same timid boy except now you carry a weapon, which you are supposed to use sometime or the other. In all probability it's some villagers gathering Gucchi mushrooms. You know they are supposed to sprout out of the ground during lightning and thunder. But let's not take chances, I will lead and if there is a firefight go easy on the ammo.'

Keeping the smoke as the direction marker, Manzur stealthily crept up using the thick undergrowth for cover. As he came up the mound, the scene that confronted him stalled him in his tracks. There, barely thirty metres ahead, in an opening around a blazing log fire, a couple of men were kneeling, while a bunch of soldiers covered them with their weapons. A babble of voices emanated from the assembly, of harsh commands and scared pleading responses. The soldiers were milling around the men on the ground and briefly Manzur was confused about their identity, for most of them were bearded. The mujahideen also had beards and quite a few of them wore camouflage jackets and trousers.

But the confusion cleared as quickly and his first instinct was to duck down and beat a hasty retreat. But, by then, one of the soldiers was turning around and, perhaps in his nervousness or imagination, Manzur thought he had been sighted and instinctively fired a long burst from his AK in the general direction, before turning to flee. The forest erupted to loud gunfire and from the corner of his eye, he saw a few people crumble to the ground. He was not sure if they had been hit or were just diving for cover. Then he turned and raced downhill, conscious of only one thing—that none of his mates were anywhere to be seen. The yellow bastards, he thought. Must sort them out for this cowardly transgression.

He heard gunfire behind him and for the next twenty minutes, he dashed headlong downhill through the scrub in blind panic. He paused finally for thought and breath, only after he was certain no pursuit could be possible. Manzur drank some water from a nearby stream and calmed his racing heart, as he inspected his torn clothes, lacerated neck and hands. Then taking a circuitous route he climbed back towards his village. So much for his mother's breakfast, he thought, as he trudged uphill cautiously. Three hours later, he was on the periphery of his village, watching from a vantage point for any unusual or suspicious activity. Finding the place peaceful, he slipped across to his neighbour's house. Then he sent for his sister and instructed her to pass word to Aslam's parents to tell him to meet up at the pre-decided RV for the meeting with Malik the next day. He didn't want to warn the parents in advance that their house was the one selected for the meeting.

In the meanwhile, he decided to address some personal matters such as reacquainting himself with the Kumar family in the neighbourhood, provided they hadn't already packed up and departed. The locals mentioned that RK was operating openly with the Army and they had seen him when the patrol had gone through the village. His sister, while denying having seen RK, told him the Army was carrying a casualty and were in a hurry to descend. Manzur eyed her suspiciously. He was visibly disturbed on hearing that RK was now operating with some Army unit. The fact that the soldiers he had briefly glimpsed wore beards, and had turned up in that godforsaken corner of the mountain in appalling weather, confirmed his fears that they were in all probability special troops.

He remembered the few instructors who had impressed him at the commando course. They were hard men he recalled—very calm, tough and self-assured—proudly wearing their maroon berets. The men would invariably set an example first, before asking the students to do anything where physical strength or risk was involved. Manzur admired their quality to walk the talk, instead of just barking orders. This, however, was definitely not good news. He of course did not know that airborne forces follow a tradition, where the senior most man must always lead in any situation where risk to life is involved.

His sister further mentioned about the two villagers who were killed. Manzur was quite distressed to hear that his fire had caused the death of two innocent civilians.

CHAPTER 4

Chakrabarti Village—Bhadarwah Hills

Ever tried. Ever failed. No Matter.
Try again. Fail again. Fail better.

—Samuel Beckett

The meeting with Malik took place at Aslam's house. The two-storey house was tucked smugly into a fold of the hills and out of sight, nestled as it was, in the harbour of thick leafy Deodar trees. It was the last cottage at the periphery of the village and the nearest house was beyond shouting distance further down the hill. Behind the house, the ground fell away in a steep gradient, with interwinding gullies and nullahs, covered with hawthorn and underbrush. The terrain constraints made it impossible for the house to be surrounded comprehensively from all sides by troops.

A few local militants entered first, followed by a tall and gaunt bearded man. After the usual greetings and introductions were over, Malik and Manzur sat down on the *gaba* blanket which had been placed on the wooden floor. The others followed suit, lounging around wherever space was available. Manzur noticed Malik was a bit edgy and comforted him with the security precautions that had been taken.

'My boys are covering all the approaches to the village,' he told Malik. 'Don't worry brother, you are our guest. Our lives before any harm comes to you.'

Malik weighed him up. His previous tenure in the Lolab valley had left him with a very poor impression of the local mujahids. They were smooth talkers, untrustworthy and deceitful, with the bulk of them fighting for personal reasons, with no clear picture of the larger goals of jehad. But this bunch of hillmen were slightly different from the ones he had encountered in the valley. For one, they were physically tougher and more reliable, but averse to risk and content to maintain the status quo. The lot needed to be prodded constantly into action, but once subjected to it, they performed better than their contemporaries in the valley. Or maybe, he thought, his bitter experiences in the valley had prejudiced him against them and, in the final analysis, the entire lot was of the same mettle. Manzur though gave him the impression of solidity, someone who wouldn't back off once he committed. Perhaps it had something to do with his military training.

Aslam, playing the host, had set down piping hot cups of tea, fried chicken and some glucose biscuits, which everyone tucked into hungrily. Once the dishes had been cleared and the preliminary chit-chat done with, Malik got down to business.

'Manzur Bhai, forgive me, but the seniors across are viewing your area very poorly. Not enough is being done to keep the jehad active. We need to show some results, if I have to get them to sanction weapons and funds for this belt. All of it is being diverted to the valley.'

'Well, we ambushed an Army column just yesterday,' Manzur answered defensively. 'The Army controls the towns and the valleys and we run the show in the mountains. What more do you want us to do?'

'I heard about your contact,' Malik replied, 'where unfortunately two innocents were also killed from the same faith. If you don't want to engage with the Army, considering your numbers are small, then clean up the kafirs in your backyard. The valley is rid of them.'

'And have the Army baying for our blood up in the hills too,' retorted Manzur. 'How do you expect us to operate if our families are vulnerable to state harassment? What exactly is it that you have in mind, brother? We will work with you if you have a plan that does not jeopardise our near and dear ones.'

'There is no plan as of yet, but Inshallah there is perhaps a target,' answered Malik, looking directly into Manzur's eyes. 'Further up the valley, at a place called Puneja, sits a small Army post. I am told it is ripe for the taking. Irfan here with me, has a brother who is a porter for the Army and knows everything and everybody on that post.'

'Tell them, Irfan,' said Malik to a short man standing in the corner.

The man stepped forward now and told the assembly what he knew. His brother had gone across to Pakistan with him for training. But once back home, the parents had put their foot down and forbidden both the boys from joining up for the fight. So the younger brother had dropped out much against his wishes, and after doing odd jobs for a while, had landed up as a porter for the Army. He was staying now in Bhadarwah and was a regular porter for lugging up rations, etc. from the roadhead to the post. He often spent the night in the post or in the village below and was well acquainted with the layout of the place. In fact, he was on very cordial relations with most of them and they had no idea of his connection to jehad. According to him, the soldiers had got complacent over time and the post could easily be attacked. There was enough cover to approach the target stealthily and enough mountains around to disappear as easily after the raid.

A joint recce of the target was decided to be carried out that night. This was Manzur's backyard and he knew of the village and the Army post. Except that he had never contemplated raiding a post. It was too ambitious an operation. Even now he was a little apprehensive about the retaliation that would certainly follow in the aftermath of the raid. But the die was cast and he couldn't possibly back out of an op, especially in front of a foreign mujahid. Later in the evening, as the sun went down, Manzur found himself with Malik and a few other fighters, across the river halfway up the mountain, heading south along an unused path that traversed right past and above the main military camp. He saw the lights in the camp below and could feel, rather than hear, the steady palpable throb of a generator. As this was the larger army base, he guessed the men he had clashed with perhaps came from the camp below.

They passed above the main town, the lights twinkling in the houses and the streets empty of people. It reminded Manzur of the time when he was a kid and a leopard had turned man-eater, claiming a few human lives. A ghastly quiet would descend over the villages after sunset and none would venture out. An insurgency environment was also much like a land plagued by a man-eating big cat. All human movement stops at dusk; a deathly silence descends over the place, as people bar themselves indoors in fear. The path now swung sharply right and climbed up diagonally. Another two hours of walking and Manzur called for a halt. As Malik sidled up to him, he pointed down.

There through the forest, barely a couple of hundred yards below, torch lights were moving on a dark strip of land. A faint murmur of voices carried up to the watching men, someone coughed and cleared his throat, the clank of a utensil being knocked against a rock, or perhaps a weapon being cocked.

'The post?' inquired Malik.

'Yes. Now we wait till the morning to get a better picture,' answered Manzur.

They settled down against the trees, wrapping their shawls around them. The nights were getting cold and Manzur only hoped it wouldn't rain, or else it would be a miserable night. The next morning, before the first roosters crowed in the village of Puneja, the team had settled down behind trees, throwing some shrubs and branches in front for camouflage. From their vantage point, they studied the target for its weak spots, the adjoining ground and the stand to drill, that was in progress, and is followed at both first and last light by most armies across the world. They counted the number of troops, the siting of the automatics and, more importantly, the alertness of the soldiers.

Within an hour of watching the post, Malik's hopes soared. It was like a ripe mango waiting to be plucked. Everything was wrong—the deployment of the post, weapons, proximity to the village providing cover and, most important, the laxity of the drills, indicating a sense of false security amongst the soldiers. Clearly, in their minds, nothing had happened and nothing would happen. He had once hit a Russian post way back in Afghanistan, but that had been a debacle. Somehow they had forgotten about the perimeter mines and the moment one of them exploded, it blew away the element of surprise, along with the man who had stepped on it. Then it was a hasty retreat, as the post guns engaged them, followed by the mortars and, subsequently, the worst nightmare, when a helicopter gunship hounded them up the hill.

Things would be easier here, he thought, no gunships for sure to deal with. Sometime later in the morning, they retraced their steps back to Aslam's house along the same path and, somewhere along the way, the decision was taken to hit the post next Friday. Other than it being a moonless night, it was also Jumma, the day of Allah.

Twenty men in all were supposed to take part in the raid. Two groups were made of ten men each, to be commanded by Manzur and Malik respectively. Malik's remaining fighters had turned up from Banihal and the Gul Gulabgarh area where they were operating and included a few foreigners. Splitting up into smaller five-men squads, the militants approached the target area from different directions the night before the raid. Except for three men, who, circumventing the village, had climbed up and stationed themselves in the forest above the post, the rest of them slipped into the village piecemeal. After the assault, the teams were to disengage and withdraw by the same route they had taken in.

The village headman was then summoned and instructed to take all the adults of fighting age and surreptitiously clear out of the village in small groups. Sometime during the night the sentry at the lower post heard some bustle at the other end of the village but, as no dogs barked, he did not consider it suspicious enough to raise an alarm. He was not to know that the muzzle of the dogs had been tied to stop them from barking. A few of them were subsequently found loitering around the cook house in the morning after the raid, helplessly pawing at their muzzles in irritation, which were still tied firmly with pyjama strings.

Just before first light, when the night is supposed to be at its darkest, the militants crept out of the now empty houses, for most of the men had taken their women and kids along, leaving the old and the infirm behind cowering in fear in one of the houses. Fanning out in the shape of a crescent moon, the militants crawled their way up to the edge of the fields bordering the post. Here they waited for the day to break. Manzur was so close that he could hear the sentries' restless shuffling. He had often been on sentry duty back when he was serving in the BSF and knew the last rotation before morning was the worst time. One just waited for the day to break to grab the desperately needed cup of tea and some food.

A little later, he heard the strike of a match as the man lit a cigarette, his mongoloid features visible in the glow to Manzur from where he lay hiding in the shadows. Enjoy it, he thought, for it's going to be your last cigarette. He heard the man unzip and then take a loud piss. Someone moved in the tent in front. There was a clanging of utensils and then the hiss of a stove being lit, the flames showing through the canvas and silhouetting the man. Manzur was fretting by now, for they had been lying doggo for the past hour or so. He wondered what Malik was up to and why he wasn't giving the signal to fire, for the camp was coming alive.

From their vantage point during the recce, the lower camp was not visible and they had planned on the raid time, basing it on what they had noticed at the smaller post above. It now seemed they had overlooked the cook house located in the main post below. For clearly some of the soldiers were up early to prepare tea and breakfast for the rest of the men. The only flaw in the plan, thought Manzur. Dawn was fast appearing, as the first streaks of light lit up the overcast grey sky. Any further delay and the raiding force ran the risk of being daylighted.

'What is Malik waiting for,' the man next to Manzur whispered.

'Not sure, brother, probably wants them to finish their breakfast,' he whispered back.

The next instant, the morning calm was torn asunder by gunfire from the right. Manzur and team joined in, firing into the tents and spraying the area from end to end. He had the satisfaction of seeing the soldier in the tent pirouette like a dervish dancer and crumble in a heap. The din of the firing was deafening as the entire group of closely packed men opened up with their weapons on automatic mode. Someone tossed a grenade. Between bursts of gunfire, Manzur heard names being called out of the soldiers on the post. A machine gun had started to fire back at them, but Manzur was unsure where it was firing from. Then somebody shouted the age-old battle cry, Allahu Akbar, and in a body the militants rose from their positions and charged.

Manzur, firing from the hip, jumped over some overturned barrels and headed straight into a small tent on the side. A soldier, wearing headphones, sat hunched over a radio set, engrossed and screaming into the mouthpiece in a strange language. While the Nepali language was unintelligible to him, the purport of the message being relayed was clear. He was reporting the incident and clearly asking for reinforcements. The soldier had to be stopped from doing so immediately. The man's back was towards him and, at point blank range, Manzur raised the weapon and pressed the trigger. A click, the magazine was empty.

The soldier had still not noticed his presence and Manzur fumbled with the knife he carried strapped to his ammo vest. Using the butt would have been quicker, but his AK had a metal folding stock and he was uncertain of its efficacy as a club, to bash the man's head. Whipping the knife out, he jerked the soldier's head back roughly by the hair and in one swift movement, sliced the neck from end to end. Driven by fear and nervousness, he kept sawing reflexively at the neck, completely oblivious that the man was long dead, till Aslam who had followed him, entered the tent and wrenched him by his collar.

'Come away Manzur Bhai, leave him alone, he is dead. The post is heating up. We need to go.'

Manzur came to his senses and picking up the radio set and the soldier's weapon, he followed Aslam out. It was each man to himself now. The camp was in shambles, with bodies and gear strewn around. He saw a fleeting glimpse of the porter, who had helped them in planning the raid, lying dead with half his face blown away by a burst. Should have stuck to portering, brother, he thought. As per plan, Manzur was supposed to climb up after the raid, but a light machine gun clattering at the post on top, was scything up the area randomly. He didn't want to catch a stray, or the gunner's attention in trying to slip past him towards the mountain behind. Left with no choice, they first went down with the aim to take a detour, slipping and sliding cross country, past the village to the road. Here their headlong flight came to a sudden halt, for coming up the road from the Bhadarwah end, at breakneck speed, were two vehicles loaded with bearded men bristling with weapons.

He knew immediately they were his old acquaintances from the last contact. Men he didn't want to entangle with. 'Turn around, turn around, brother,' he told Aslam, as he swung his weapon and let loose a long burst towards the vehicles which had now come to a screeching stop on the road below. Should keep their heads down, but not for long, he reckoned. Using the cover provided by the terraced fields and the crop, they managed to reach the forest cover. Linking up with his three men who were still blazing away at the post from the edge of the forest, they headed upwards.

Retreating up the hill, they ran into a Gujjar coming down with his cattle. Commandeering one of his ponies, they loaded it with all the looted weapons and the radio and headed further up. In a few hours, they hit the top and grabbing something to eat from the nearest Gujjar hut, they swung north along the ridge line, after warning the Gujjars to expect the Army in their wake. Certain that pursuit by the Army would now be futile, especially as the weather had packed up on the heights and visibility was practically zero, Manzur finally allowed himself the satisfaction of a job well done and let his mind drift to more pleasant images of his future young wife, Razia. The thought of her warmed his heart and stirred pleasurable feelings between his legs. Love or lust he was unsure, but he decided to rush back to Jora Kalan immediately to formalise the marriage, with or without her husband's consent.

Women and weather were unreliable, he mused, and must be enjoyed immediately as and when the opportunity arose, for who knew when they would turn for the worst.

'*Allah Ta'ala*, some respite,' he muttered to himself, 'there's not been a dull moment since I became your servant. This jehad sure is a busy business.'

CHAPTER 5

Bhadarwah Hills

A Snider squibbed in the jungle, Somebody laughed and fled,
And the men of the First Shikaris, Picked up their Subaltern dead,
With a big blue mark in his forehead, And the back blown out of his head.

—Rudyard Kipling, *The Grave of the Hundred Head*

RK's local intelligence had confirmed that the ambush had been the work of none other than Manzur, who had accidentally run into Harry on his way to the village. In fact, the SP also knew the names of the other three members of Manzur's party who were along with him that day.

'All local boys and classmates,' the SP told Harry. 'Apparently they have been going around the villages boasting about the fight and embellishing the tale. Bad luck my friend, for our plan was sound. If you hadn't run into those woodcutters, you would have been smugly lying in wait for Manzur in the village.

And he in any case was coincidentally heading your way. Ill-met on the ridge line, for it was the wrong place and the wrong time for you.'

Harry was busy the next few days collecting intel from some of the local soldiers he had dispatched back to their villages up in the hills, while the evenings he invariably spent with the SP, plotting and planning how to square the account with Manzur. A couple of stiff drinks down and the SP's Hindu Dogra chauvinism would emerge. A student of history, he firmly believed the erstwhile Dogra rule had been the best thing for Kashmir. Being at the fag end of his career, he was prepared to take chances and often bypassed official channels and procedures. In his own way, the older man had given Harry a free hand.

'Just go out and operate with a free hand and a free mind,' he mentioned to Harry. 'I will take care of any consequent issues.'

In the SF, they firmly believed one had to be aggressive enough and quick enough, if one wanted to stay on top of the game. However, unbeknownst to Harry, while he planned, Manzur was already ahead in the game and the next shocker was about to unfold. A week or so had passed after his contact with Manzur, when Harry was woken up early one morning, by the irritable whirring of the field telephone. He looked at the machine askance, wondering why couldn't these phones ring like normal telephones. It was the Assam Battalion Adjutant, Rohit, a course mate of Harry's at the military academy at the other end and clearly in an excitable state. He told Harry to move post-haste with his men to one of their platoon localities at Puneja village, about 5 km further south up the valley. The post was apparently under attack.

Harry checked his watch—the luminous hands showed it was just shy of five. He glanced through the curtain-less windows at the faint glow accentuating the silhouette of the dark surrounding mountains, heralding the advent of daylight shortly. He remembered it was a Friday, not that the days of a week mattered in an op environment, but today India was playing a cricket match and he was looking forward to watching it in the Assam mess. The distant faint sound of a raging gun battle carried across the sleeping valley, with automatic fire, intermittently interspersed with the dull thud of a grenade explosion.

It took Harry ten minutes to round up fifteen men, who fell in any odd way—sleepy-eyed, tousled hair, carrying their personal weapons and ammo pouches. Harry briefed them quickly for there was very little to brief. They were going in as the cavalry to salvage a rapidly deteriorating situation.

'Play it by the ear,' he told them. 'This might be an uphill fight, on a narrow front. So let the guys in front engage. And look lively and sharp boys, it's bandit country all the way.'

He was pleased to note some of the men were hurriedly stuffing sanitary pads into their battle pouch pockets. It amused him to think that suddenly after the last contact, the sanitary napkin seemed to have taken precedence over food and water. En route they picked up a soldier from the Assam Battalion HQ, who knew the way to the post. The platoon post was located on a spur about a twenty-minute walk uphill from the road. They drove at breakneck speed in two vehicles, disregarding all vehicle drills that should be followed in an insurgency area. Harry kept his fingers crossed that they were not ambushed, as the narrow dirt track was hemmed on both sides by terraced hills, with rippling high corn crop providing plenty of cover.

Perfect ambush country, thought Harry, if someone wanted to have a go. The entire stretch of the road, after leaving town, had the potential to be turned into a killing ground. An advantage of height, the possibility to engage from both sides of the road, along with limited manoeuvrability, drastically tipped the balance in favour of the ambushing party. None would live to tell the tale, thought Harry, as he scanned the hillside, weapon cocked and cradled in his arms for a quick response. Harry wondered if it could be Manzur and company at work here, or some other militant group taking advantage of an easy target. Whoever it was, sure had the balls to attack a defended post. The hills it seemed were heating up suddenly. Two back-to-back contacts and both initiated by the opposition was not a good sign though.

The fear of being ambushed was soon replaced by the dread of overturning or crashing into the hill, as they took the switchbacks at reckless speed. The overloaded vehicles skidded and groaned in protest, as the drivers pushed them to the extreme of their performance. Harry tapped the young driver on the shoulder and told him to slow down.

As they got off the vehicles to start the climb on a bridle path, they came under sporadic fire. Harry quickly weighed his options—to hang around on the road or to climb the twisting well-worn path, which in all probability would be covered by a cut-off party to stop any reinforcements from that direction. However, as no pebbles seemed to be doing a tango around him, he pressed on, for the fire didn't seem to be accurate and was more to dissuade any reinforcements from reaching the beleaguered post, rather than to inflict casualties. Soon the firing was desultory, from various directions, and from the sound, some of it was receding which indicated the withdrawal of the raiding force. The militants it seemed were breaking into smaller bodies to disperse in different directions, making pursuit difficult. Harry passed through the village which was deserted and arrived at the post above or what was once a post. For right now it was in shambles. He clearly wasn't prepared for the sight that met his eyes.

Tents perforated with bullet holes looked like giant canvas sieves, dangling precariously on broken poles and blowing lustily in the strong morning breeze coming down the mountain. The guy ropes had been cut, equipment lay scattered and a deathly silence engulfed the post. The only conspicuous sound was of the tent flaps violently flapping in the wind and the rustling of the chest-high crop of corn in the fields below. Everywhere and everything bore a mark of the ferocity of the attack.

Harry gingerly made his way from tent to tent and the sight left him boiling with rage. The cook was in a kneeling position, with his head jammed in a large utensil, shot while making tea. A fire still simmered under the utensil and Harry gently moved the utensil, with the man's head still stuck in it, before extinguishing the fire. The last thing they needed were the tents set ablaze. He didn't have the heart to wrench the man's head out of the utensil, fearing a glimpse of his face. Another soldier was lying at the entrance to the cook house tent, which had collapsed on him, with his legs protruding out. He was wearing rubber bathroom slippers and one of his little toe nails had red nail polish. Probably came to collect his morning cup of tea and got a bullet instead.

In the signals tent, muted sunlight streamed in through bullet holes and the operator seemed to be asleep, with his head resting on the desk. On closer inspection Harry discovered his neck had been sliced open from ear to ear like a melon. It was a huge gash—a crude and an unprofessional job, thought Harry. It seemed the killer in his nervousness had overdone the cutting. Probably used to killing goats and buffaloes by halal, he had gone about applying the same amount of unnecessary pressure on a man. Or maybe the guy wanted to decapitate, but ran out of time. Warm blood was still seeping out of the wound and a huge pool of thick coagulated blood had collected under the head.

Harry tried to imagine the last moments of the operator, as he frantically called for assistance. The man must have been still transmitting SOS messages when his executioner entered from behind and finding him preoccupied, decided to polish his knife on the man's throat. Decapitation was always preferred if possible by the mujahideen over a bullet when dispatching an infidel. For not only did it get you bragging rights, it also took you a notch higher in attaining a place in paradise. After all, anyone can kill with a gun, but it takes a different kind of courage to close in with the enemy and cut his throat with a knife. Also the sheer brutality, the gruesomeness of slitting a throat, takes the act of killing to a different level. A few other bodies were lying in different areas of the camp and a vast amount of arms and other stuff had been taken away by the militants, including the standard ANPRC-25 radio set. Except for the absence of arrows and tomahawks sticking out of backs, it looked like the Apaches had come calling in a Hollywood western.

The only sign of any worthwhile resistance was from the LMG position, in front of which two militants lay dead. The first guy, wearing a light-blue, half-sleeve sweater, had half his head blown away and was lying barely ten feet away from the LMG position. Harry wondered at the degree of hatred, madness or sheer courage that would have driven the man to charge a LMG bunker head on, spitting at certain death. Some of the men on the post were still missing and the saving grace was a sentry post slightly ahead at the adjoining camp, which kept up a withering fire throughout the engagement. The Gurkha NCO (Non Commissioned officer) narrated the events to Harry. Apparently the raiding force came at night and parked themselves in the village. They tied the muzzle of the dogs and all the locals, especially males of fighting age, were told to evacuate the village in anticipation of the soldiers' retaliation that may follow after the raid. The NCO pointed to the dead militant and told Harry he lived in the village below and was a porter for them.

'Nice guy, he would eat and smoke with us and then turns out to be the most ferocious of the lot—charged the LMG position alone. Who knew he hated us so much and that he was a member of the Harkat-ul-Ansar.'

Nobody was sure if it was the handiwork of the Harkat or of the local *tanzim*, Hizb-ul-Mujahideen, under the able leadership of the ex-BSF Manzur Ahmad.

It was, however, a classical raid and commenced at the crack of dawn. Harry could see the platoon post was clearly badly sited, and because of terrain constraints, split into two smaller defended localities along a spur fifty metres apart. Sitting in a straight line on this narrow spur, the deployment of the automatics in both the posts was not in an interlocking arc of fire. The ideal position would have been further down the spur where it flattened out, but most of this space had naturally been consumed over the years by the village of Puneja.

The lower post became the one most vulnerable, with a steep gradient to its approach from the south providing adequate cover, screened as it was by the adjoining corn fields and the village below. Harry noticed the 2IC of the unit, who had also arrived, standing alone to one side and surveying the carnage. His distraught expression was rapidly crumbling into grief and Harry got the impression he might just break into tears any moment. He was absorbing the scene and trying to fathom the enormity of the disaster and how it could have come about. Harry, feeling sorry for the man, sauntered up to him and summarised the sequence of events.

'The lower post must have been invested from three sides and fired upon, Sir,' he told the 2IC, 'while the mujahideen called the soldiers on the post by their names, suggesting they stop the resistance and lay down arms. Clearly inside information was available to the militants, Sir.'

Having heard the account from the men on the post, Harry tried to latch on to concrete images of how the incident must have unfolded. When no one surrendered, the mujahideen must have lost patience, realising the clock was ticking, as daylight beckoned and the post was also finally stirring itself from slumber into violent activity. The chant of 'Allahu Akbar' must have rent the morning calm as the militants finally dashed out of cover, firing and overran the camp. The soldiers at the post had undeniably become complacent and been caught by surprise. It was estimated by the troops on the post that fifty to sixty militants must have taken part, from all the noise they made, but Harry's guess was that they were probably no more than twenty to twenty-five. In the fog of battle, everything is confusing, accentuated and enhanced. Time slows down.

The 2IC chatted up a few of the men and heard their version of the raid. He seemed in a daze, as he tried to make sense of the disaster and was concerned about accounting for the missing men. Harry told him the village was involved—the same village which was living off his largesse in rations and medicine had stabbed him in the back. A lesson should be taught, and in his anger, Harry suggested mortaring the village. The 2IC, a mature half colonel, gave him a deep look pondering hard over the matter, then sensibly controlled the urge to follow his suggestion. So Harry requested if he could borrow their two-inch mortars. He badgered the man for some sort of a retaliation but the 2IC was more concerned about evacuating his wounded, accounting for his missing personal, some of whom were emerging gradually from the adjoining corn field, and facing the Brigade Commander, who had the reputation of turning up at all the hot spots.

Harry had already fallen foul of him once after his ambush incident, when he was hauled up for apparently concocting a story. The Commander was convinced Harry had gone about shooting civilians in cold blood. Perhaps, thought Harry, the Brig in his younger days aspired to join the SF and failed his probation. For he made no bones about his dislike for the SF, calling them rogue cowboys shooting from the hip.

'You tread carefully, while you operate in my jurisdiction,' he had warned Harry. 'Look at the mess you have created for me and this is not even a disturbed area. Trigger happy fuckers!

I will get to know the truth from intercepts and village gossip. Rest assured, I will have you court-martialled, if I find out you have shot them in cold blood.'

Harry was tempted to tell him he had also collected a casualty in the bargain, in this so-called cold-blooded killing spree, but decided to keep his counsel. After all he had seen better men come to grief in operations, for standing their ground and answering back to a senior. The Army had zero patience for insubordination, especially in a combat zone.

Shortly, as expected, the Brigadier arrived and surveyed the carnage with a jaundiced eye. Harry hung around at the periphery watching the proceedings. Having had one bad experience, he didn't want the Brig accusing him of raiding the camp, impersonating as mujahideen! The Brigade Commander pacified the 2IC and insisted the report must not mention the camp was raided and overrun. He was equally worried about his dossier getting smeared. A chopper hovered overhead and it reminded Harry of a crime scene under investigation that one sees in movies. Then the Brig turned and noticed Harry lurking around under the trees and seemed surprised.

'You have a knack of turning up at all the wrong places,' he told Harry.

'I want this avenged,' he continued, addressing both the officers. 'I am throwing in all the troops and have requisitioned for a team from your unit too,' he said, looking at Harry. 'In the meanwhile, I suggest you climb up and search while the team will link up with you as and when they arrive.'

Harry endorsed the Brigadier's feelings and was briefly tempted to offer him his unwanted advice to mortar the village as a start, but then decided against it. Doda district was, after all, not a disturbed area and the suggestion would only reinforce the Brigadier's view about Harry being a trigger-happy killer. Harry believed in the Sicilian saying: *Lu Sangu Lava Lu Sangu*—Blood washes blood. However, he had a feeling this was going to be again one of those large retaliatory ops which bring a lot of grief to the troops involved and bugger all in terms of results.

No army worth its salt likes to be beaten, certainly not the Indian Army, especially if it has a fighting history of over two centuries, spread across the world. But like any traditional army, with heavy manpower, its planning ethos tends to get mired in troop inundation as an answer for any op. Creativity and imagination in planning is often suppressed, and the training schools advocate adherence to time-tested military doctrines. The map is dotted with reds and blues indicating troop positions, with no thought to contours or the terrain. Remarks like 'where can the bugger go now' are bandied about and the staff officers exchange smug looks in the comfort of the ops room. No wonder, the old British army had a derisive slang for the *staff wallah*s—'the Gaberdine Swines'.

Harry climbed for an hour and settled down to wait for the team. An uncomfortable night was spent in the open and he was glad when daylight broke. It was all thickly-forested country and with no maps or prominent landmarks it became difficult for the team to link up with them the next day. As they had carried no water or food in their haste to provide succour to the post, the wait now became a bit of a burden. Finally the two parties met after hours of radio chats and false RVs, amid rising frustration on both sides. Harry decided to split the team with each taking different routes, and for the next five hours, they steadily climbed with back-breaking weight.

Harry was surprised at the size of the mountain, for it didn't seem to end and he felt it wasn't going to end in a hurry either. A quick look at the map confirmed they were heading up to over 12,000 feet. When they finally hit the top, it was drizzling and a menacing heavy mist, thick enough to be sliced with one's hand, enshrouded all, limiting visibility to a few feet. Confusion reigned supreme, with the trigger happy troops having climbed up from different points of the hill, coming perilously close to shooting each other. Next morning as the mist lifted, Harry discovered they were on a large rolling plane dotted with Gujjar huts, all vacated in a hurry. It seemed the Gujjars had got wind of the attack, or had been warned by the departing militants as they went through. What puzzled Harry was how they had managed to disappear without a trace—with women, kids and all their livestock.

The few peaks around still carried snow and a large path cut across the pasture to disappear down the other side. The Brigadier turned up in the afternoon with a pony caravan carrying winter clothing and food for his troops. Whatever his faults, Harry thought, physical fitness was not one of them. This was apparently going to be a long haul and he too moved forward to collect his supplies. The Brig tried to brush him away as he had just enough replenishments for his own boys. As SF teams don't report directly to the immediate one up chain of command, they are often treated like transit troops—to be used and abandoned when resources are scarce and loyalties in question.

Harry had faced this attitude before but decided to stand his ground, pointing at his wet dress and demanding food and clothing for his men. The Brig had none and in his irritation told Harry to fuck off the mountain. With an insolent look and a withered salute, he made a hasty departure before the Brig had time to change his mind. It had been nearly thirty-six hours of constant motion, inadequately dressed for the altitude, with practically no food or sleep. From experience, he knew the birds would have long flown the coop. This was only an exercise in futility and it was better to get off the mountain before his men started falling prey to the inclement weather and altitude.

His departure was not taken lightly by the Brigadier, who must have immediately sent a report higher up the chain of command. This was confirmed, as the first thing Harry was told on coming back to camp was that he was to report to the General commanding Delta Force at Batot 'asap'. Harry's name seemed to be appearing too often in the situation reports going up to the Div HQ from the Brigade. And they didn't make good reading—civilians shot, post raided, insubordination, a rogue contingent footloose in the hills.

Harry was ushered into the tent that was the General's office-cum-residence. He took the initiative and opened the volley with some straight talk. The General heard him out patiently and then, instead of giving him a dressing down, offered a cup of tea. With a few words of encouragement Harry was dismissed.

CHAPTER 6

Pahalgam Valley—Kashmir

Do not rejoice in his defeat, you men! Although the world stood up and stopped the bastard, the bitch that bore him is in heat again.

—Bertolt Brecht

The man looked down the thickly-forested spur, his eyes taking in the sweep of the distant mountains and then fell on the path below. The dirt track, which had appeared out of the woods at the base of the hill, lost itself after a while in the chaotic maze of the village ahead. Poplar trees marked the countryside and the tin roofs of the houses stood lacklustre under an overcast sky. The snow melt had been early and the pastures were flush with wild flowers. Blue gentians and yellow daisies were sprouting out of the soggy ground and the air was pungent with the smell of pine needles and white lilac. Small streams, fed by the melting snow further up the mountain, sloshed down playfully in rivulets—the clear waters gently eddying, to collect in multiple cascading mini pools.

A river, the colour of dull chocolate and swollen by the rains, noisily ran through the middle of the village, and disappeared round a hill in the distance. It's sound faintly carried up to the man as he inhaled sharply the crisp mountain air. He sighed. Beyond those mountains barred with snow, somewhere far away lay his home. He was not a man given to sentiments easily, for he had long ago forsaken his kith and kin for a bigger cause. As a votary to his religion, he was an adherent to violence in the glorious pursuit of jehad. But there were times when a certain smell or a sight would briefly stir a long dormant memory—buried deep in the recesses of his mind—of a place he once called home. This was one of those moments.

He was unusually tall for these parts and sparsely built, with a stern hawk face dominated by an aquiline nose and thin lips. Lips that rarely entertained a smile and were now cracked due to constant exposure to the harsh mountain elements. A flowing beard and shoulder length hair gave him a romantic wild appearance, in consonance with the trade he practised—a killer of kafirs. There was command written in every line of his physical bearing, and like most natural leaders of men, he was taciturn by nature. His name was Hamid-ul-Turki and he hailed from the north-west frontier of Pakistan. He belonged to a small community that traced its roots to the early Turks, inhabiting both sides of the border.

Turki was his *nom de guerre* in the Arabic jehadi jargon—his *kunya,* or his fighting name—and he had been in the business of violence for most of his adult life. Knowing no other trade, he was in all practical sense a 'career' mujahid. Turki had undergone jehadi training based on the three pillars of *Tarbiyat* (training), *Haj Habi Tablighi* (religious indoctrination) and jehad (holy war). It was incumbent on those who completed the entire course to wage the holy war anywhere in the world where his religion was thought to be in threat. While Turki took his orders from handlers in Pakistan, he liked to believe that he fought under the banner of Islam and not as a pawn of the Pakistani state, in pursuit of their political gains in Kashmir. Following the muezzin's call, haranguing the faithful from the *minbar* of a mosque, he had drifted from conflict to conflict across the world.

By the time Turki arrived in Kashmir, years of violence had defined his character, moulding him into a cold hardened fighting machine. The man was as indifferent to his death as he was remorseless for those so-called kafirs, whose early demise had been at his hands. He had been involved on and off for many years now in the so-called *Jehad-e-Kashmir* and had been hand-picked by the *tanzim* he belonged to, the Harkat-ul-Ansar, which was in cahoots with the Pakistan's ISI for a specific operation. The plan was to kidnap a few foreigners and take them hostage, so as to leverage a trade-off for four top Paki militants incarcerated in Indian jails.

The first attempt was a failure as the team tasked with the job landed up by mistake in the Charar-i-Sharief shrine and unwillingly got embroiled in a face-off between a Paki mujahid by the name of Haroon Khan alias Mast Gul and his cronies ensconced in the 700-year-old shrine of saint Sheikh Nooruddin Noorani and the Indian Army lying in cordon outside.

Mast Gul, with his penchant for publicity, kept the media glued to his antics, while the Army in deference to a holy place, frustratingly waited for direction from higher quarters.

The delay gave the militants time to boost their numbers and nearly a hundred hardened killers gathered, emboldened by Mast Gul's brazen defiance of the Indian Army. They were confident that the Army would never assault the holiest of shrines, teeming with so many innocent believers. The SF sniper teams, however, accounted for half a dozen or so militants in the interim. The two-month long impasse finally came to an end when the militants, in their desperation to break out, torched the ancient wooden structure. As Charar-i-Sharief burned, Mast Gul got away in the confusion to subsequently surface back in Pakistan as the hero of Charar. Some said the militants escaped by hiding in the fire tender trucks, which were rushed to extinguish the blaze, slowly engulfing the market and the timber houses, while others theorised they wore burkhas and escaped detection in the melee that followed the fire.

Whatever the methods adopted, the militants had lost numbers and the original hostage team paid its price too for getting embroiled in the scrap. From the dwindled numbers, a band of twelve hand-picked fighters from the north-west frontier and the Punjab in Pakistan were entrusted under Turki's command. The dirty dozen extricated themselves from the mayhem of the moment and cautiously made their way further to thc Pahalgam heights. To ensure nothing could be traced back to a Paki hand in the planning and execution, a splinter unknown group was formed by the name of Al Faran.

Pahalgam was the only place in the strife-ridden Kashmir valley where one could always run into unsuspecting foreigners—tourists visiting to experience the beautiful locales and excellent treks the place had to offer. Pahalgam was full of pristine meadows, high altitude lakes and glaciers, all spread out in the shadows of rugged summits. One could climb north-east towards Sheshnag and Amarnath, head north-west into alpine pastures or camp in the quaint mountain villages of Kolahoi and Aru. Hundreds of sheep and frolicking ponies grazed sweeping pastures. Wild-looking Gujjar men in traditional turbans tended to livestock while their women folk, adorned in colourful clothes and jewellery with the hair done up in numerous pleats, attended to domestic chores and pink-cheeked children. This then was the place Turki had in mind for making the planned abduction.

A year earlier, the kidnapping of two foreigners by local militants had gone off smoothly, though both had been released two weeks later. The model had worked perfectly and only needed to be replicated.

The cancellation of the first operation was playing heavy on Turki's mind, and he was under tremendous pressure from across the border to ensure things went according to plan. They were already a couple of months late and time was running out. In a few months winter would set in, disrupting to and fro movement across the border and also make the heights almost impossible to sustain a body of men on the run. Leading a few of his fighters, along with some local Kashmiri and Gujjar militants, he descended the mountain to round up a few foreign trekkers who were camping around the Aru valley. The ragged bunch of men, heavily bearded and armed to the teeth, went down the rough mountain path which leads to the Lidder river.

Barging into the first couple of tents pitched on the grassy meadow, the militants rounded up six foreigners, and leaving their women partners behind, marched them out into the gathering dusk. As night settled over the mountains, the hostages found themselves being herded further into the mountain fastness, with the militants setting up a gruelling pace. Most of the hostages had had a rigorous day of hiking and were yet to acclimatise to the height, suffering mild headaches as a consequence. Shaken by the suddenness of the untoward events and anxious with fear, they ascended the unknown dark mountain with gloomy thoughts.

Sometime before daybreak the group arrived at some isolated Gujjar *dhoak*s (huts) and settled down for rest. Built of timber and stone, more for solidity than comfort, the *dhoak*s were like medieval dwellings and used by the Gujjars as summer settlements, when they migrated up the mountains in search of pastures for their livestock. The hostages were now shoved into one of these huts and the only exit locked and guarded by armed militants. Realising by now that there was no point in making any resistance, each hostage wrapped himself in the meagre clothing he had and withdrew into whatever space he could find in his befuddled mind and around the tiny spartan hut. Most were suffering from mild altitude sickness for they were at nearly 11,000 feet.

The hostage tourists slept fitfully on the damp and cold mud-plastered floor while a biting wind howled through the cracks in the walls. As cattle usually occupy the front part of a *dhoak,* with their owners sleeping behind on a raised platform, the place was also flea-ridden and stank of cow-dung and animal urine. One man, however, an American named John Child, remained vigilant and impervious to the discomfort. Stretched out uncomfortably in the dark, his thoughts were very different from what the others were thinking. Escape, rather than hope, was foremost on his mind. He knew that the best time to escape was always in the beginning of the capture and with every successive day those chances reduced exponentially. Having made up his mind, he waited for an opportune moment, which presented itself in the next couple of days.

Feigning an upset stomach, the American stepped out from the *dhoak* into a pitch black freezing night and made a show of squatting behind some boulders. Then, with his heart beating an alarming staccato and a prayer on his lips, he gathered up his trousers and slipped downhill quietly, expecting a burst of fire from behind any moment. Soon he had put a large distance between him and his captors, while his fellow captives slept unaware. After covering a certain distance, he turned uphill, knowing that the search, whenever he was discovered missing, would focus on the lower slopes. Worn to exhaustion, he was spotted the next morning aimlessly loitering around on the frigid heights by the security advisor to the governor, who had decided to spin around randomly over the mountains in a chopper.

A brilliant piece of flying by the ex-Air Force pilot ensured that the American was scooped up from a cliff edge and flown back to Srinagar for debriefing. The American was extremely gutsy in taking his chances for had he been caught, nothing short of death would have been his punishment. Men like Turki are not known to forgive transgressions easily, but then sometimes fortune favours the brave. His escape, however, now added grief for the other hostages, who were immediately bundled and marched out to another location.

The remaining five—two Brits, an American, a Norwegian and a German student were now taken on a desperate hide-

and-seek game in the high mountains. Moving constantly from one Gujjar settlement to another, the party managed to stay ahead of its searchers. The constant movement made it difficult for the security forces to pinpoint their location and they followed the random wanderings of the group on their maps in frustration. The group would be sighted by some Gujjars in Kolahoi village one day and then suddenly drop off the security forces radar the very next. Patiently, the hunters waited, tracking the movement with the trickle of intelligence that came down the mountain, as the Al Faran tramped around criss-crossing their path often, but never staying more than a few days at any one location.

Winter was round the corner and up on the heights the weather was closing in. The group was gradually running out of steam and ground. Finally, information came in that the group crossing the Margan top had dropped onto the other side and entered the remote valley of Warwan. The constant moves in the last two months, the long marches over inhospitable terrain, along with the local fare of cornmeal roti and cabbage had taken a toll on the hostages, wearing them down to a shadow. All of them were in a physically ragged state and in crying need for some rest. They desperately needed time and a place for a bit of rest and recuperation. The village of Sukhnoi at the tip of the valley was an ideal place to hole up and Turki decided to pitch camp and take stock, while he decided his next plan of action. Messages had been sent back to Pakistan regarding the difficulty of finding any more safe hideouts and of continuing indefinitely in the present situation. If the Indians hadn't capitulated so far to the demands put forth, then a decision had to be quickly taken about the future of the hostages. Turki now awaited further orders.

CHAPTER 7

The Hills—Bhadarwah

You can have vengeance or peace. But you can't have both.

—Herbert Hoover

Meanwhile, as Al Faran with the hostages made their way towards the Warwan valley, miles down south across the Chenab river, Harry was seething with anger and itching for retribution. To have the gumption to attack an Army post and get away with it set a dangerous precedent. More posts would be attacked, convoys ambushed and the state of affairs could degenerate very rapidly to the levels of insurgency existing in the valley. The terrain here was also far more conducive to guerrilla warfare and an emboldened enemy could play merry hell with the security forces strung across isolated posts and section-level pickets. Retaliation had to be immediate and in equal measure. But how?

The only way to do it, in Harry's opinion, was to sprinkle a small body of SF men across villages up in the hills, supported by air for replenishments, supplies etc. While the concept of small team ops was briefly tested and disallowed in Sri Lanka, for fear of the team getting surrounded and cut off in the jungles, it was highly doable in the Pir Panjal. But then, it's the crisis that demands the reaction and by standards of militancy, for the powers that be, the conflict in the Doda hills probably hadn't reached the 'required' crisis levels for trying new concepts as yet.

An attempt was made to raise a civil volunteer force by training and arming the minority community so that they could defend their homes. But this throws up other foreseeable concerns—primarily the difficulty of disarming the lot once the threat was over, leaving a motley bunch of armed novices free to thrash out personal vendetta in the old Wild West style. The group also becomes vulnerable targets for militants, who, sensing a threat to their authority go for them with a vengeance.

Harry couldn't get the picture of the signalman, with his neck slit like a goat in his own backyard, out of his mind. He was reminded of the US Army's motivational catchphrase used during the Vietnam war: 'Don't get sad. Get even.' From his Sri Lanka experience, he knew only violent aggression got you respect from a belligerent opposition. The Tamil Tigers had a healthy respect for the Indian SF and generally gave them a wide berth, getting into a fight only when cornered. For there is nothing more psychologically devastating than to know that your opponent, if angered, would pursue you to the gates of the netherworld.

But then the magnitude of the exercise dawned on him and a wave of despondency threatened to engulf him. The canvas was too large, the mountains too big and the handful of militants, scattered over a vast forested acreage, were like the proverbial needle in the haystack. He reckoned the return on effort, as compared to the valley, was probably three to one and it easily took three times more effort to get a kill in the Pir Panjal mountains.

A number of men under Harry were locals from villages around and came back from leave with tales of desperate reprobates pillaging villages in the name of jehad, led by none other than Manzur Ahmad. One of the men from the team, Havildar Saifullah Khan, belonged to the village of Jora Kalan and had been making regular trips to collect intelligence. A slim tall man who was also extremely fit, Saif had the gift of the gab and often conducted the namaz sermon for the men. He was highly intelligent, resourceful and had often managed to extricate himself from tight spots when confronted by militants back in the village, with some glib talking. According to him, after the raid on the post, Manzur and his cronies had gone back to their old haunt and were running a parallel government in the remote distant valley. Harry realised the standard practice of sending a fighting patrol up the mountain and hoping to get lucky was not going to work. It was such a long way off that the jungle drums would be playing out the reception by the time they were half way to their destination. Novel ways had to be found to maintain surprise and get close enough to engage effectively.

A seek-and-destroy mission was planned, and to ensure surprise, Harry decided to go covert. The main party under the Team Commander would tail them, staying behind and above on the mountain, in radio contact at all times, to bail them out in case things got too hot.

However, their timelines to arrive at the designated rendezvous went for a six when the climb turned out to be of prodigious proportions, taking over fifteen hours. At some deserted Gujjar huts, four local soldiers along with Harry, changed into the traditional *salwar kameez* and stripped themselves of all military accoutrements, carrying just their personal weapons, ammo and a small radio. Harry checked their get-up and felt confident. Two were Muslim and two Hindu and while on closer scrutiny they wouldn't pass muster with a genuine militant, hopefully the impersonation would sail through with the locals. The only concern was the stubble Harry carried instead of a thick beard. The pseudo militant gang was ready to disengage and roam free to make contact.

Within an hour, Harry's squad lost contact with the main party in the thick forest and he dithered to enter the twin villages higher up, supposedly packed with a large body of trigger-happy killers, without the backup. The next twenty-four hours were spent going up and down in search of the rest of the team. They had carried no water or food and the exercise by the evening started to get bothersome. In spite of being hillmen and at the peak of their fitness, they found their speed slowing down, except Saifullah Khan who was indefatigable and was driving all of them along. Saif seemed to be more worried about clashing with a genuine militant group than the rest of them were and insisted that a link-up with the main column was a must, as the valley was infested with mujahids. Sometime in the evening they ran into a couple of Gujjars, who were inordinately polite and cautioned them to be careful, for they had heard through the grapevine that an Army column was in the area. That's the end of surprise, thought Harry.

They had a quick meal of rough and thick cornmeal roti and white butter at a Gujjar habitation comprising a couple of *dhoaks*, where Harry was introduced as a senior Paki mujahid on a surveillance tour for jehad. Harry sat aloof looking all solemn, a man weighed with the responsibility of command, while the daughter of the host, a very pretty young girl served them food. Before leaving, Harry tipped the patriarch of the family, a tall venerable looking ancient with a flowing white beard, a hundred rupees and just for devilment, conveyed through the men that he had a pretty daughter and one would certainly be coming back to pay her a visit.

'And the next time, hospitality shouldn't be limited to just food. This is the custom of our people back home in Pakistan.'

There was an ominous silence as the words sank in and with a lecherous glance at the girl, Harry stepped out into the gathering darkness pleased at having given the Pakis a bad name for whatever it was worth.

A bitterly cold night was spent in the forest and Harry was glad when the sun crept over the surrounding crests. Sometime in the afternoon they finally met up with the rest of the team and Harry refused to move anywhere till they had some rest. It had been a very stressful and demanding twenty-four hours. As night descended, the rebel village of Jora Kalan across the valley came alive to the agitated barking of dogs and numerous torches were seen heading out of the village. Very soon, the last of the torches disappeared up the hill. The dogs lost interest, reverting to a state of somnolence, and the natural quietude and darkness of the place reasserted itself. The militants had vacated the area as per Saifullah Khan. They were aware of the presence of the patrol somewhere in the valley.

As surprise was lost, decision was taken to abort the operation and roll back. The next morning, Harry decided to pay the village a visit. Leaving the local boys behind, he went across with a few men. The village of Jora Kalan was a collection of fifty houses, each with its piece of adjoining land carved out in steps and given to cultivation of beans and maize. The latter was ripe for harvest and was standing the height of a man, with long parrot green leaves, wet and glistening with the early morning dew. It struck Harry if anything beat the irritation of walking through a shoulder-high corn field, then it was definitely forging a way through a ripe sugarcane field. The latter with hard stems and rough leaves often bruised the face and the exposed limbs.

He recalled the many nights spent training, when they would fly out in choppers from their mountain base, slither down in some fields next to the Yamuna river, followed by an infuriating march through cane fields to a pre-selected target—an old British railway bridge over the river. It was sugarcane country and produced the mother of all sugarcanes. He remembered the stem was stout and tall like a bamboo and the leaves were as sharp as a cleaver's edge.

Jora Kalan was a pure Muslim village and not as prosperous as some of the villages further down the mountain. At some stage in the not-too-recent past, population and land pressures must have driven people further into the mountains, for the village gave the impression of an improvised ad hoc settlement. Forest had been cleared and a side of the mountain terraced out for cultivation, with rough mud and timber houses precariously clinging to its side. The nearest roadhead was at Bhadarwah or further north at Thatri, both taking a full day's march.

Such a place made a perfect haunt for desperadoes and renegades shying away from the laws of the land.

The wizened headman, hauled out of his home, confirmed the presence of Manzur and other militants and that they had vacated in a hurry the previous night, as the Army was somewhere in the forests. He also mentioned that Manzur had his eyes on a married girl from the village, and having forced the husband to divorce her at gunpoint, was in the process of getting married to her forcefully when the alarm was raised about the Army. The ceremony remained incomplete as Manzur had to take flight, but not before mentioning that he would be back soon to complete the ritual formalities.

The girl was a complete emotional wreck, Harry was told, as she quite loved her husband. So, thought Harry, that was the hullabaloo he had witnessed the prior evening—a family drama in the small community with the neighbours pitching in with their two penny bits and the bloody dogs also joining the fray, till the threat of the patrol had suddenly disrupted the proceedings.

'Well, present the couple,' said Harry, to the headman. 'If her love is true, then she will get the man she deserves. For I am the judge and jury for the time being.'

Shortly, a young couple was escorted into his presence. Tousled hair and sleepy eyed, they stood there looking forlorn and unsure, exchanging looks with all and sundry who had collected. The young girl, having figured out quickly that Harry was in command, darted shy furtive glances at him from time to time. Harry had a look at Manzur Ahmad's object of love or lust and came to the conclusion that he had good taste in women. She was short and sturdy, but pretty, with a fair complexion, running more to muscle than fat because of the hard life these people led. But what appealed to Harry most, and must have perhaps also appealed to Manzur, was the woman's strong character. She came across as bold and strong-willed and it surprised him how she had fallen for the man next to her. For he looked meek and in their relationship, it was quite obvious the girl wore the trousers.

Harry addressed the headman who it seemed was also the local *kazi*, judge and the *maulvi* for the small village community and was the one who had been conducting the marriage ceremony the night before. The girl confirmed she had no intention of marrying Manzur, a militant, and would like to be remarried to her ex-husband. A quick ceremony was carried out under the aegis of Harry's guns and in double quick time the couple was declared man and wife once again. Harry sat through the simple ceremony of the *kalma* recital, smug at the thought that, in his own way, he had at least paid back Manzur. Trivial though it may seem, losing his love was certainly going to unsettle him for the time being. Some sweet tea and fried chicken followed and then Harry told the young couple to pack up and leave with him. For he was certain Manzur would be out of the woods in a rage and any further divorce and re-wedding would only leave the poor girl very confused.

They linked up with the men who had been left behind and Harry told Saifullah to switch back into civvies. Handing him a radio, Harry instructed him to head back to his village and to inform him in case the militants converged back to the area in the next day or two. Saifullah had been doing this often and Harry didn't see any risk in the undertaking. The timing for their radio interaction twice a day was fixed and in case of any emergency, Saif could call in anytime, as the base radio would be on a constant listening watch till he was out. The next morning, instead of going cross country, they openly marched back down the village path which wound its way above the stream, through the Deodar forest back to the BSF post at Jai and then down to Bhadarwah.

The first day Saifullah Khan made his regular calls but thereafter, for the next three days, there was complete radio silence. Harry started to get a trifle concerned. Just when he was planning to take a patrol up in search, a pony caravan with a few relatives in tow, carried him down the mountain to the Assam Rifles post in Bhadarwah. Harry walked into the tent which served as a makeshift Medical Inspection room. One look at Saif and he knew the man's time was up. There were tubes sticking into him and his face carried the pallor of death, as if he had done twelve rounds in the ring with a professional heavyweight. But the face was the least of the worries—according to the RMO (Regimental Medical Officer), his kidneys were ruptured and most of the ribs broken. He was passing no urine and there was injury to his lungs too.

The grievous damage, both external and internal, was clearly unrepairable and to see such a healthy and strong man broken like a trampled twig, left Harry shocked and speechless. He had seen enough dead and bullet-ridden men, but a badly battered human fighting a losing battle with life had a profound effect and moved him deeply. He could barely comprehend the words of the brother, who in a whisper narrated the sequence of events. The militants had paid the village a visit the very next day and having seen Saifullah home once again got suspicious. As a rule, Muslim soldiers were not troubled by the militants but here was one getting more leave than was usual. Perhaps they also intercepted a few of the radio conversations, because they kept questioning him about the radio set.

The militants tortured him for the next twelve hours, running over his body the heavy wooden cylindrical tool used for flattening clods during ploughing. Only after he was comatose had they relented and left, but not before threatening dire consequences to the family if they made any efforts to help him. After two days, the brothers finally mustered enough courage to haul him over a pony and carry him down. In his state, the journey must have been hell on a pony and probably hastened his deterioration. Saifullah now opened one bruised, heavily swollen eye and looked at Harry pleadingly.

Harry found it difficult to meet his single bloodshot gaze, for his mind was a whirl of emotions and self-justification—was it his fault to have sent him back alone? Rushed ill-conceived plans and what was the consequence? A botched pseudo op. He bent close to Saif, who wanted to say something.

'I have a family to look after, Sahib,' he said in a pained hoarse whisper. 'While as a soldier one is ready to die, I didn't know it would be like this and so early. Manzur was present, but it was a foreign militant who worked on me viciously and wanted to get his hands on the radio set. It is in the cattle shed, Sahib. In their conversations, I heard Manzur mention about a job in the Warwan. Something to do with escorting a party of foreign militants and hostages across the Chenab.'

With the rest of the family looking careworn and helpless, Harry held Saif's limp hand and made the right utterances of encouragement, promising retaliation. But Saif was beyond listening. His children, a boy of ten and a younger girl, looked terribly distraught. They had perhaps witnessed the father being tortured and heard his cries of pain, and it had clearly effected them. Neither child could now muster courage to look at their battered father and they hung around silently in one corner of the tent, holding back their tears. Harry stood there, looking down at the tortured, mangled supine form of what was once a fine specimen of a man, with a normal life, till Manzur came along to stamp on it like one would do on an insect. Briefly, he toyed with the idea of going back up the hill to Manzur's village to vent his ire on some of the relatives, but dropped the idea immediately. Doda district had not been declared a disturbed area and any violence would be treated as a criminal offence. The last thing he needed now was a few more IPC sections added to his already running charge of murder.

Then he thought of sending RK up with a squad of his own men in covert. While his men would hang around at the periphery of the village, RK could be let loose for a calibrated violent response. Just enough damage to man and property to get the message across to Manzur. But then he knew how unpredictable RK was, especially with a gun, and more so when it came to Manzur. He was like a misguided missile, zipping around aimlessly, while all one could do was to watch helplessly from the sidelines.

The distant sound of the chopper grew loud, breaking into his reverie. It landed next to the road on a small grassy patch, in a whirlwind of dust. Havildar Saifullah Khan was immediately evacuated to the military hospital in Udhampur, where he slipped into coma.

CHAPTER 8

Base—Udhampur

Beware that you do not lose the substance by clutching at the shadows

—Aesop

Harry decided to cease the punishment he was subjecting everybody to by planning these relentless ops, often on poor intelligence. It was a case of shadow boxing, thought Harry. All posturing and no substance. Saif's torture had shaken his confidence and he decided to pause and review his modus operandi. Senselessly climbing hills and hoping to get lucky was not helping him and it was only wearing the men down. This kind of random wandering and the odd opportunity ambush on the ridge lines in the Kashmir valley had often got results earlier, but the Pir Panjals were a different kettle of fish. For one, the mountains were way bigger and more spread out, other than a much lesser density of militants per sq km.

One would have to be extremely fortunate to clash accidentally with Manzur and company.

A few weeks later, as he sat discussing ops with the SP, who had grown quite fond of Harry and was always full of ideas and imaginative ways to get at Manzur, he received a message recalling him back to the unit base at Udhampur for a forthcoming op. The SP was genuinely sad to see him depart and promised him lots of actionable intelligence when he got back. A four-hour drive and Harry was in Udhampur, eagerly looking forward to getting his fill of good food and some decent company. The first thing the CO informed him about was Saif's demise. Harry was visibly disturbed and put in a request to drop out of the op, for he wanted revenge and didn't want to be pulled out of his current location. The heat had to be turned on Manzur and this op would only divert his focus elsewhere.

He firmly believed that in insurgency operations or in war, soldiers must adhere to the law of *lex talionis* or blood for blood. If you were in the difficult business of trading in lives, then the only way the balance sheet remained green was by inflicting more damage on your adversary. Revenge was also a great motivational force multiplier. So far it had just been a vendetta played out between RK and Manzur, with the Army watching from the sidelines and treating any militant as a threat to be eliminated. But now, with Saif's inhuman and unsoldierly death at the hands of Manzur, it had somehow become personal. Very, very personal.

The CO gave out the briefing for the two teams which would be participating in the new op. Despite wanting to focus on Manzur, Harry couldn't make his CO change his mind about leaving him out of it. The officers from both the teams were present and there was much bonhomie as they were catching up after months. Alpha team had been floating around in north Kashmir, while Harry's Bravo team minus his troop had been in and out of Udhampur operating in the Pir Panjals. Not much info was available on the op except the bare facts that the Al Faran, a hitherto unknown militant group, had abducted a group of foreign trekkers and had finally been run to ground. They were in all probability holed up in a small village at the northern tip of the Warwan valley.

Intercepts confirmed that they might try to break out of the valley, for the constant aerial surveillance they were under was making them jittery. The local HM commander from Bhadarwah, it seemed, had been roped in to provide them the next hiding place. Movement of militants in and out of the Warwan valley was therefore expected to increase, and the Corp HQ wanted to ensure this ingress and egress from the valley was denied to them. The Al Faran was to be boxed in and contained in their mountain redoubt.

Hostage rescue scenarios were also discussed among the few SF teams which had arrived from the various countries to which the hostages belonged. The SAS and the German GSG-9 teams were the most experienced in hostage rescue ops and were leading all the discussions. They went over the terrain pictures and the target intelligence, and sensibly decided that any rescue op would be a risky proposition, and if an attempt was to be made, it should be carried out only by the Indian SF which had been operating in that terrain for years now. They were generous enough to offer any specialised equipment the Indians might need.

'So the hostage rescue bit is out of the window for the time being,' said the CO. 'We only need to carry out aggressive patrolling to discourage southward militant movement. If that pushes them back over the mountains into the Pahalgam valley, good for us—it makes rescue ops that much easier. Do not, gentlemen,' he said and looked at each officer gravely to emphasise the point, 'in your enthusiasm, advance up the valley to seek an encounter. Heads will roll if a hostage comes to grief because of our straying too close.'

'Ideally,' he continued, 'we should ensure this HM commander, some guy called Manzur Ahmad, does not make contact with the abductors, for he is the local man and other than knowing the ground is also supposed to provide protection.'

'I have crossed path with the man, Sir,' interjected Harry abruptly. 'Wily sort, with a couple of his erstwhile school classmates in tow. A BSF deserter, so has some military background.' The restrained undertone of anger in his voice was palpable to all as he continued. 'Sticks to the villages higher up and often joins hands with the Harkat for the odd larger job. He is the man who ambushed me, subsequently tortured Saif, and in all probability, is the man who raided the post at Puneja. I am more interested in his scalp then Al Faran or the hostages.'

'Active bastard, this Mazur chap,' answered the colonel. 'Need to square up with him then, considering its two–love in his favour. But make sure you focus on the job in hand and don't get emotionally swayed to take some unnecessary risks just to get even with him.'

'Just before he was evacuated, Sir, Saif mentioned a snatch of conversation he overheard while they were working on him, about Manzur going off to Warwan in connection with this

Al Faran business. Well, couldn't figure out what he meant then. It all fits in now. With Manzur heading in the same direction, I am certainly in the op then,' continued Harry. 'Who knows we might run lucky, Sir, after all Warwan is not exactly his home wicket. Also, if you permit, I would like to take along an ex-colleague of Manzur from his BSF days, who had been operating with me earlier. In fact, they are childhood friends and from the same village. To cut a long story short, they hate each other and I am still discovering the depth of their enmity, for apparently they have been murdering each other's family members on a regular basis. Just like the north-west frontier where some of these blood feuds could go on for generations. This guy—RK—could be of help if Manzur is involved. The only problem is we will have to borrow him from the police and I am not sure if the SP will be too pleased to let him out of his jurisdiction. You see, Sir, he is supposed to behind bars on charge of multiple murders.'

'Oh! Is that so?' the Col answered, a worried frown creasing his forehead, 'Not sure if it's advisable to have a psychopath on the loose with an automatic supplied by us. I think he is better off in police custody Harry. And you can connect with him once and if you go back to Bhadarwah.'

'Well Sir, he has been operating with the troop for some time,' answered Harry, 'and it's always good to have a local. Bit of a loose cannon, but he speaks the lingo and his personal antipathy towards Manzur drives him to take risks which I wouldn't allow my men. Useful to send him down to the villages to gather intel or his ability to enter a house without raising any suspicion.'

'You take his guarantee Harry in that case. Although despite his obvious usefulness in hunting Manzur in Doda, I am not sure what he can contribute in a different area, especially to the op that we are going in for,' said the Col. 'Also make sure you keep an eye on him. Don't want him adrift in the villages with a loose tongue and morals, chasing skirts and bullying the locals on our backing.'

The afternoon saw Alpha team disappear down the road in a convoy of vehicles, to be in position in Pahalgam by night, with orders to start climbing at the crack of dawn towards the Margan top. Bravo team meanwhile spent the night in comfort at the base, to be airlifted to their op location the next day.

Squatting like some giant bloated dragonflies, the two Air Force MI-8 choppers were slicing the early morning air with their rotor blades, as the ground crew hurriedly ran the checks on their machines. The CO along with the men boarded the choppers and Harry settled himself next to a window. The birds taxied a short distance and then, in tandem, with an anguished whine of the engines, they were airborne. What by road would have taken six hours of travel and then a walk was covered in twenty minutes as the choppers crossed the town of Kishtwar and dropped height.

Following the contours, they flew low over the river dwarfed by mountains on both sides. Harry looked out of the window at the mountains slipping by and so close that he feared it might just tempt the militants, if they were lurking around in the forested hills, to open up with their AKs at such an easy target. The Russians in Afghanistan had often lost gunships and troop-carrying choppers to small arms and rocket fire as they flew low in the valleys. Harry always preferred choppers with the rear hatch open, as it gave one a better picture of the world below and a fighting chance in case fired upon from the ground.

A little later, the river disappeared from sight and the scene below changed to that of withered fields and scattered houses. In a cloud of soft dust and swishing dried husk, the bird settled down. Disgorging its human load, it took off immediately clearing the LZ and turning over the river. The second chopper followed in its wake to land heavily with a thud. Following SOPs for such heli-borne ops, within minutes the two birds linked up in formation, to fly back to base. Receding rapidly, they were soon tiny specks in the huge expanse of the valley and long after they had disappeared from sight, the faint sound of their engines still lingered in the air.

Harry, watching the departing choppers, was reminded of Sri Lanka again, where one had a fleeting sense of vulnerability and isolation the moment the air link was severed. While one was airborne, the mind could be at ease, in the comfort that things were out of your hand—que sera sera—and it was after all the pilot's responsibility to get you down in one piece. However, the moment you were on terra firma, one had to switch on all of one's senses and take charge pronto. But that was Sri Lanka, where mental ease was just an occasional episode, in a general drama of high stress existence.

To the men watching on the ground, it seemed the pilots were in an undue hurry to depart. Perhaps they were worried about their breakfast getting cold.

CHAPTER 9

The Warwan Valley

You don't appreciate the full flavour of life until you risk losing it.

—Wanda Rutkiewicz

The crisis had been going on for a couple of months when the beheaded body of one of the hostages, the Norwegian Hans Christian Ostro, was discovered, with the word Al Faran carved out on his chest. The American hostage Child's escape had emboldened the others, especially the Norwegian, who had become brazenly defiant over time and was proving to be an uncooperative prisoner to handle. He had made a few abortive attempts to escape and Turki finally lost his patience one fine day. Taking him back across the Margan top into the Pahalgam valley, he personally executed him there. The other captives got the message and simmered down. Henceforth, there would be no further attempts at escape and none would even harbour the thought. Turki knew he had sorted the freedom movement for the time being, for they would accept miseries and privations now with the stoicism of a cow standing in the rain.

The discovery of the dead hostage, however, created a stir, making headlines internationally and led to a frenzy of activity in the government and the Army. Rumours of where the hostages were being held flew thick and fast. They were in the Pir Panjals, it was said by some, while others surmised they could have crossed over into Himachal, as the heat was too much in the valley. Another school of thought believed the remaining hostages may have already been taken across into Pakistan or killed and buried, leaving the Norwegian's body in the open as a message to the government. Whatever the truth, the team was about to find out.

The Warwan valley at an average elevation of 7000 feet is a narrow piece of land, running 30 km end to end, no more than 3 km at its broadest. It lies north-east of the town of Kishtwar and is hemmed in by high mountains, with Kashmir on one side and the Zanskar on its western flank in Ladakh. Unlike the Kashmir valley, which is bestowed with the balanced proportion of distance and height, lending an effect of sublimity, the Warwan has a more savage appeal. There is nothing soft about the place and its people, and the feeling is of sheer majestic ruggedness. The remoteness of the area had ensured its isolation so far and it was the first time the Army was venturing there. The only security force presence was a BSF post, further south at the mouth of the valley.

The general modus operandi followed by the ISI planners running the Kashmir desk was to dictate the pace of the insurgency and the direction. You stepped up attacks on the security forces in a particular area, knowing the predictable

Indian tendency to immediately inundate it with troops. So you invariably kept a lying up place, a side valley or a town which had been incident free and where the mujahideen could bolt to, in case they were harassed by the Indians forces. These areas were usually off the security forces radar because of little or nil militant activity. The Warwan was one such place.

Harry could see the valley tapering at its northern end and snow-clad peaks in the far distance. Poplars lining the paths and fields provided a green relief in a landscape rapidly turning dull ochre in anticipation of the harsh winters. At the northern tip of this valley, under the snow-laden summits of the mountains that rose up to nearly 14,000 feet, clinging precariously to its rocky side, sat the last impoverished village of Sukhnoi. It was where Al Faran apparently now held the hostages.

The moment Harry's team landed, a firm base was established in a couple of houses and the first to get cracking like always were the signals and mess detachments. The team was split into smaller sub-units and patrolling commenced with a vengeance. Orders were very clear—not to cross beyond Inchan and spook Al Faran into doing something desperate with the hostages, but to deny them free access down south into the Pir Panjal massive. Knowing the quality of intelligence one receives from higher HQ, nobody took the Al Faran story seriously. In fact, the higher the source of the intelligence, the more unintelligible it generally was. Harry had once received intelligence in the Lolab from the Div HQ, and they had apparently received it from higher up, about a confirmed border crossing giving the exact date, time and strength of the party. He was also given the names of the two Paki SSG officers in command. Amazing, thought Harry, as if the source was sitting in the Pak planning room and during a coffee break, excused himself to make a call to his Indian handler, to pass on the info.

Alpha Team, in the meanwhile, had commenced their climb from the Pahalgam valley to the barren Margan top, from where the path running north-west drops into the Warwan. They had the same orders—not to probe too deep but show enough presence so as to dissuade any militant movement back into the Kashmir valley. On the map, for all practical purpose, the Al Faran was bottled. But Harry knew the cordon was far from effective and neither had they the capability nor was the terrain conducive for a hostage rescue bid.

While frenzied patrolling was happening at Harry's end, with everybody questioning the sanity of this self-affliction, the Al Faran leader Hamid-ul-Turki, getting impatient with the waiting, dispatched two of his lieutenants with a Gujjar guide, who had been with them from the time they had crossed the border. He was a Shamshabari Gujjar from way up north in Machhal and specialised in border crossings, but here he was too down south to be of any use. Their orders were to make contact with Manzur Ahmad, who had been instructed to meet them in a village lower down the valley in Warwan. He would then guide the whole team along with the hostages, to the next safe haven, somewhere south of the Chenab river.

Setting off early in the morning, the two Al Faran militants along with the Gujjar followed the village path that wound south along the river. It was an easy downhill walk and they felt good to finally get out of the stressful atmosphere that had been building up over months, especially in the impoverished village where they had been holed up for many days now with the hostages. While the abduction had gone off smoothly, over time the strain of managing the hostages was telling on everyone. Turki had been high strung and short-tempered ever since the American hostage escaped and then the Norwegian had pushed his luck too far with him. The remaining four foreigners seemed to have reconciled to their fate, adapting well to their surroundings and the hardscrabble existence. Relations between the two parties had improved significantly after the Norwegian's departure and a friendly bond seemed to have sprung up between them. Unbeknownst to the captors and the captives, it was classic Stockholm syndrome coming into play. Then the chopper had turned up over the village, disturbing the status quo, circling all the while from morning to evening like a patient bird of prey. Happy days were over and Turki had driven the hostages back indoors, doubling the guards in fear of a rescue attempt.

The three of them had barely crossed Inchan village when a local crossing them from the opposite direction gave the bad news. The Army was everywhere and if they continued any further on the path, it would be at a grave peril. The Gujjar immediately left the path and swung up into the hills, heading for the forest cover available higher up the slope. It was the beginning of their troubles, for they had barely hit the tree line, when a patrol was sighted climbing up in their direction. They then went higher and deeper into the forest, losing sight of the valley floor, before turning south again, to traverse the mountain flank cross country.

For three consecutive days and nights, the trio tried to break through the Army cordon in their attempt to reach the RV fixed with Manzur. The only bottle of water, carried by the Gujjar, ran out on the second day and for food they survived on a handful of dry fruits each had carried. The Gujjar seemed to have a mortal fear of losing height and going back down to the valley, for he was relentlessly driving them higher and higher, where finally the mountains became precipitous and no tracks existed. But the Army was omnipresent—in the forests, down in the villages and even high up the treacherous slopes, where no trees grow and only the Himalayan eagle soars in the chilly wind currents. From a distance using binoculars, they would often spot the lean bearded men, up a ridge line, down in the nullah or silhouetted on a crest up some craggy height.

Sensitive to the ridicule he may be subjected to by the two Paki militants, the Gujjar guide subtly warned them about the soldiers they were up against. These men were different, he told them, and he was not going to take any chances. His sudden fear of the Army surprised the two Al Faran militants, who, in all these days together, had never seen the man shy away from risk. The dread he felt for these men, for which he gave no explanation, was somehow contagious and seemed to affect the other two in their fatigued state. For neither overruled the Gujjar, when he shot down their suggestion to attempt a breakthrough at night.

'They are more alive at night than during the day. It can't be done,' is all he said.

For, while they noticed some of the patrols openly roll back to the villages further down as darkness beckoned, the Gujjar however, knew better—it was just a ploy and a body of men would have stayed back on the heights. And the dogs could see in the darkness. It was not only the Army but also the savage weather that they had to contend with. They were hard men, but even hard men have limits and the elements were stacked well against them.

Manzur, who had finally made radio contact with them on the second day, tried his best to guide them through the safest routes, but it was not easy to follow directions in an unfamiliar thickly-wooded mountainous terrain. Frustration started to rise on both sides and finally, tired and hungry, they cracked. Throwing caution to the wind, sometime in the evening of the third day, the two Al Faran militants decided to descend to the village of Dasbal.

The Gujjar guide stood his ground, gazing intently in thought at the silent habitation spread below. Smoke from various cottages hung in the still air like white ribbons, as the odd wicker lamps came alive to the advent of the rapidly approaching darkness. Then shaking his head gravely from side to side, he quietly turned and traced his steps back up the mountain. Years of high-risk border crossings had honed his sixth sense and he felt the powerful presence of danger waiting for them in that peaceful looking hamlet below, like a predator waiting silently for its prey.

The bearded soldiers, wearing black bandanas, were of a different breed and the Gujjar had run into a similar lot earlier on one of his border crossings up north in the Machhal sector. Of the six mujahideen he was guiding on that occasion, only he had lived to tell the tale. They had crossed the LOC on a moonless night, while the snow was still sitting thick in the nook and corners of the forest. It was the first infiltration of the season and he had hoped the Army may not be expecting them so early. They crossed without any mishap and were a day's march across the border, breathing a sigh of relief and thinking the worst was over, when they had walked into the killing ground. In fact, the Gujjar recalled, it wasn't just one killing ground, for as they fired back and scattered, the whole hillside had come alive with soldiers.

That's when it dawned on him—there were multiple ambushes and no path, spur or ridge was safe. Information of their crossing must have been relayed back, for clearly this bunch was waiting to lay out the reception. Movement, however minimal, was fraught with grave danger. Controlling his urge for flight, he had crawled into the hollow trunk of a tree and lain doggo for the next four hours. From his hiding place he could hear the crisp commands, the static of the radios and the intermittent signature SF style, short two-round, double-tap fire. For the SF followed the old gunfighters' rule—'Anything worth shooting is worth shooting twice. Ammo is cheap, life expensive'. The mujahideen who had managed to scatter, were systematically tracked in the forest and hunted down. And what surprised the Gujjar most was that in spite of losing a soldier, the rest of them didn't call off the search, but only renewed it with vigour. Vengeful bastards, he thought.

While the Gujjar hesitated to mention it to the two foreign mujahids, this bunch, he knew from experience, was generally shy of operating in built-up areas, preferring instead to operate in isolation on the heights, covering the oft used Gujjar trails on the spurs and ridge lines. They worked in small numbers, could sit immobile for days in ambush and live rough in the wild. Roaming at random or on basis of intelligence, they would descend suddenly on an unsuspecting quarry like a pack of hungry dogs. And once contact was made, by Allah they stuck to you like a leech to drop off only after enough blood had been spilt. And even if you did manage to extract yourself from the engagement, they either went after you like a pack of starved wolves, or, if the occasion demanded, promptly split into pairs to ferret you out, spreading across the mountain in pursuit, like a malignant cancer.

'Don't go down, brother,' he turned and made one last feeble attempt to dissuade his colleagues, locking eyes with the older man and nodding his head as a Gujjar would, to reinforce his point. 'We can still go back and try another day.'

But he knew it was futile, for they were adamant and wouldn't heed his advice. In reality they were too far wasted to reason. Hunger, cold and fatigue had got the better of them, overwhelming their sense of self preservation. Whatever the tangible reasons, sometimes, the path that you take inadvertently, leads to your destiny. And their destiny was waiting for them in the village below.

'You can stay here or go back,' said the senior man derisively, 'It matters not. We are mujahids, brother, not gutter rats scuttling about in fear. We haven't come all this distance to practice running. We are done with it. Our fate is in *Allah Ta'ala's* hand now. You can join us in that house, if you do get over your scare.'

The Gujjar, at the end of the day, was in for the money and not for the cause. In fact, he wasn't even privy to the overall plan but had an inkling of what was afoot over a period of time. While he had been paid handsomely, in the final analysis, no amount justified losing one's life. He had a wife and kids to support back in the village and their memory beckoned him now. Suddenly he felt very tired and sick of the whole thing. He had had enough and wanted to go home.

'In that case, *khuda hafiz mohtram*,' said the Gujjar, giving a sad parting smile, as he turned and went back up the hill.

They watched his receding figure, till it disappeared from sight in the forest. Then, selecting the first house on the periphery of the village, the two Paki militants went down hurriedly for some hard-earned rest and food.

The incessant radio conversation with the Al Faran members to figure out their location was making Manzur extremely jittery. So much talking on the radio was asking for trouble with the Army, which would certainly be monitoring the radio traffic. In fact, the Army had been listening into the conversation. However, the signal strength often dropped because of the mountainous terrain and a garbled picture was emerging from the snatches of conversation that could be understood. The purport of the message was clear—a meeting was in the offing. But where, when and between whom, was impossible to say. If one was at a height, with a clear line of sight, radio intercepts could often be misleading. The clarity of the reception was no indicator of the distance to the source of the transmission.

It was getting late in the evening and Manzur had been going up and down the mountain for the past couple of hours, trying to figure out which was the house mentioned by the guest mujahid. The man at the other end had a distinctly Punjabi twang and sounded tired and disoriented, for he kept saying the same thing—that they had just arrived and were ensconced in a house next to a nullah. Manzur was getting a trifle irritated with the man's intellect—he just kept repeating the same landmark—no name of the village or any other distinguishing geographical feature. He wondered if the man was deliberately giving out bare minimum directions for fear of the Army's interception or he was plain dumb.

Just when Manzur decided to call it a day and spend another cold night in the open, he thought he recognised the house. From high up, he spotted a solitary dwelling at the periphery of a village, with a shallow nullah running behind it. Well, he thought, one last attempt and if this one is also the wrong house, then it is over for the day and clearly Allah had ordained otherwise. He made contact on the radio and described the house and its environs. He heard a brief conversation in the background, as the man probably verified the details with the owner of the house and confirmed positive. But Manzur wanted to be certain before he went down.

'Chuck some wet wood in the fire,' he told the man, 'and if the smoke thickens, I have you nailed.'

From his high point, Manzur saw a lone figure come out of the house and disappear into a small shed. A little later, he saw the thin hanging ribbon of smoke burgeon in girth and volume as it bellowed out of the chimney, like a chugging steam engine straining uphill. Manzur heaved a sigh of relief. He turned to his close friend Aslam who had accompanied him from Bhadarwah, and had been with him through thick and thin.

'Stay put here and wait for me, Aslam bhai,' he said. 'No point both of us taking the risk. In any case, I plan to get them out of the house and back up in the mountains.' Then he pressed the transmit switch and sent a terse reply to the man at the other end of the radio.

'Hold your fire, brother. I am coming in.'

Finally, nearly twelve hours after he had first made radio contact with the Al Faran men in the early part of the morning, Manzur linked up with them, albeit very reluctantly. For, like the Gujjar guide, he too had a premonition of death and deep down in his guts knew it was a cardinal mistake to be leaving the heights. With the hills buzzing with Army patrols like an agitated beehive, going into the village was clearly fraught with imminent danger.

CHAPTER 10

Warwan

But we sleep by the ropes of the camp,
And we rise with a shout,
And we tramp with the sun or the moon for a lamp,
And the spray of the wind in our hair

—James Elroy Flecker, *War Song of the Saracens*

A day earlier, Captain Chauhan, radio call-sign Shaukeen, had come down the mountain and was looking forward to some rest. A short stocky officer with a rustic sense of humour, he was inordinately proud of his Rajput lineage and the fact that he was the fourth-generation male of the family to serve in the Indian Army. In jocularity, after a few drinks down, he would claim descent from the famous eleventh-century Rajput ruler, Prithvi Raj Chauhan. Shaukeen was a strong adherent to the old infantry dictum—'Don't run if you can walk; don't stand if you can sit down; don't sit down if you can lie down; and don't stay awake if you can go to sleep'. Temperamentally designed for the finer comforts of life, he followed a live and let live policy, except when provoked; then, as he maintained, his Rajput blood came to the fore and woe betide anyone who blocked the way.

The captain was now busy tucking into a hot lunch, something he had been dreaming of for the past twenty-four hours while he had been up in the harsh mountains. But before he could finish the meal, he was disturbed by an agitated local, claiming vociferously that one of his goats was missing and he suspected the Army for its disappearance. Shaukeen gave him a mouthful, lecturing him on the morals and integrity of the Indian Army before dismissing him. What followed subsequently can only be explained as predestined. In the evening, as he stepped out of his tent, he heard the mellifluous tinkling of bells and turning, saw a large goat grazing contentedly. Summoning two of his men, he told them to return the goat to the local, whose house was across the nullah, and to admonish him for suspecting the Army for such petty pilferage.

When the men opened the front door, for the polite custom of knocking before entering is absent in insurgency areas, three bearded, long-haired men sat in front of the hearth, with a pile of corn flour rotis between them and their AKs resting against the wall. There was surprise on all sides, the goat was promptly forgotten as both parties scrambled for their weapons and in the time that it takes to switch on the safety catch, a gunfight ensued. Shaukeen heard the gunshots and arched a worried eyebrow. His first thought was that the boys had got into an argument with the owner and decided to draw. And if that was the case he was certainly going to sack the senior NCO on the spot. However, the firing escalated and a little later, one of the men came running back, panting in an excited state, to report the presence of the mujahideen. Gunfire echoed as the second soldier on site continued to engage with the militants. He was alone and no time could be lost.

Night settles early in the mountains and by the time Shaukeen turned up at the encounter site with the rest of the team, it was getting dark. By his estimates, he had just about fifteen odd minutes before darkness engulfed them all and the element of escape swung significantly in favour of the militants. Never a man to dither too long over hard decisions, he decided to warm up the fight with a few rounds from the rocket launcher.

The 84 mm Carl Gustav delivers what in the boxing jargon is called a 'haymaker'—a knockout punch. It is the infantry man's last means of dominating a fight, the largest piece of ordinance in his arsenal that he can carry on his back. If it's an unwieldy weight to carry, the results more than compensate when used in combat. The weapon has proved its worth from the glacial heights in Siachen to the dank tropical jungles of Sri Lanka and it has never let the user down. The loud bang of the weapon, while jarring to the eardrums when fired in training, is pure music when done so in war. Needless to say, the SF just loved the weapon.

However, they were conscious to use it judiciously, for it had the potential to dictate a firefight's outcome. Used too early in the fight, it could compel the opposing party to disengage from the contact, especially if you wanted him to continue being in an advantageous position. Fired too late and you gave the opposition time to spread out, thereby reducing the efficacy of the weapon. Few opponents could withstand a volley of the high explosive rounds from the weapon and still be good to fight. This bunch wasn't going to be an exception either. Giving just enough distance for the warhead to arm itself, Shaukeen gave the order to fire and to aim for one of the windows, from where a lot of fire was coming on them. Two rounds in succession tore through the night, the loud bang reverberating in the narrow confines of the valley.

The distance was so close that debris of wood and stone flew in the air to land on the firing party. The guns fell silent on both sides immediately, as if the RL, like a big brother, had stepped in to put end to an unsavoury argument. An uneasy hush now descended into the vacuum created by the absence of all the small arms noise before. The only sound was the ringing in the ears and the rush of blood, as it coursed speedily to calm the adrenaline charged body. Shaukeen took a deep breath and surveyed the damage with a professional eye. Well, he thought, if the fuckers can take that and still be up for a fight then he might as well roll up the show and go home.

Briefly he toyed with the idea of waiting it out till morning before entering the smouldering ruins, then realised that his training had taken over and he was already moving, weapon cradled in the shoulder, senses alert, stepping across the threshold and taking what is called a leap of faith in building intervention drills. In the end, the only way to clear a room is to enter it, and the first man in, enters with his heart in his mouth and a silent prayer on his lips. For it takes a lot of courage to confront an unknown situation, in a confined space and that too in total darkness, knowing fully well that grievous harm awaits you on the other side. You are dead as a door nail if the cornered man is still breathing with enough strength to wield a weapon.

Shaukeen took a cautious step in and squatted, peering into the dark rooms beyond to get his eyes accustomed to the darkness. The room was black as sin. A dark figure silently sidled up, squatting next to him.

'Hello,' whispered Harry, 'selfish bastard, having all the fun alone.'

Harry, who was finishing his search for the day, had decided to roll back to his base via Shaukeen's location. He had just about hit the troop tents when the firing erupted, followed by the twin big bangs of the RL. The sentry on duty briefed him on the run as he rushed to the contact and caught up with Shaukeen.

'Don't like the look of it,' Harry whispered. 'Wish I could follow what a Sufi saint once said.'

'You and your sayings, Sir! So what did he say?'

'I went in and left myself outside,' answered Harry, getting up.

Harry realised the risk they were taking and his mind started painting doomsday scenarios. While imagination can help some if controlled and constructive, it can be ruinous for those who allow it to run riot. Harry reminded himself something he often did in such situations, especially every time he went for his parachute jumps, that when it feels scary to jump, that is exactly when you jump. Otherwise, you end up staying in the same place your whole life.

He recalled vividly an anecdote that had brought home this point to him very early in his career. He had gone with his team for the annual refresher jumps to Agra and was told a contingent of the President's Body Guards (PBG) would be joining them for the jump. One has to be over six feet to join the PBG and basically the job entails providing a ceremonial guard to the President. One of the last surviving cavalry units, they are great horsemen and cut a fine figure in their resplendent dress on parade. Big men with big moustaches, they would have been categorised as heavy cavalry in the days of horse soldiering. Every member of the PBG is also a qualified paratrooper. However, like most big men, they don't really enjoy parachuting.

Perhaps the hard impact on landing because of their heavy weight makes it an unpleasant experience. Whatever the reasons, parachuting other than getting them the coveted wing to adorn the uniform, had no practical or operational purpose whatsoever. Most men managed to avoid it, if they could. If facial expressions could be considered a fair reflection of the inner turmoil, then this bunch clearly was jumping after a long hiatus. Fear and apprehension was noticeable on every face.

The sticks were intermingled and the men boarded the aircraft. While the SF guys indulged in the usual nervous bantering, the PBG men remained morose and quiet. Moreover, while the latter cut a fine figure on a horse, with a swirling polo stick or tent pegging at some equestrian display, here in a military aircraft, they struck a discordant note. Towering over their compatriots from the SF, they looked ungainly and unimpressive in their drooping ill-fitting helmets and sagging parachutes. Harry's stick was the first to exit and he was on the ground as the AN-32 banked, circled gracefully and then steadied, to line up for the second drop.

The port stick commenced their jump. Harry stood watching as tiny figures fell out, to be whiplashed in the slipstream, before the chutes mushroomed and drifted away. One, two, three…he counted and then a long pause. Clearly an emergency or someone had hesitated. For every ten-second delay, the gap could be a thousand feet or more between the jumpers, depending on wind conditions. The tail end was certainly sailing out of the DZ (Dropping zone) he thought.

Having deposited his silk, Harry had decided to investigate, as the delay had been inordinately long for some of the men to have landed outside the drop zone. As he neared the control tower, he heard raised angry voices. An ugly spat it seemed was in progress. Two groups of hostile men faced each other. The aggression seemed to be emanating from the SF quarters, while the PBG men stood around unsure, embarrassingly shuffling their feet. At the fore was Havildar Girwar, a black belt, accosting a huge man with admirable handlebar moustache. He was timidly listening to the choicest of expletives being hurled at him by Girwar, who just about reached his shoulder.

'All right simmer down,' Harry intervened, 'what's the matter?'

'Sahib,' said Girwar, 'this oaf was in front of me in the stick and as he came to the door, he just froze and holding onto the centre rod, anchored himself like a rock, and I couldn't budge him an inch. And then, unbelievably, the sister fucker decided to make himself comfortable and promptly plonked down at the edge, hanging his feet like he was on a joy ride. I first tried to shove him off and then had to climb over his shoulder to exit. The next man also followed suit and we nearly entangled. My chute deployed so late I thought I was a dead man. Most of us landed outside the DZ. Rajinder went into the high power cables across the road. Such a big man and such a small heart, Sahib. Now, cowards can't wear those moustaches, not where I come from. So the choice is very clear to him—either he shaves off his moustache now, or I will thrash him first and then shave it for him.'

Harry had a faint idea what may have happened but asked the big man all the same.

'How do I explain it, Sahib,' the man demurred. 'You see Sir, I am jumping after years and I have never liked the experience. Perhaps I don't have a head for heights. This time I made a cardinal mistake, for I started to think. I should have jumped from the aircraft when the dispatcher said go, but I hesitated. Then the longer I paused, the more I imagined, the more uncertain and unsettled I became, till my legs turned jelly and fear engulfed me so comprehensively, that I just had to sit down. I don't know, Sahib, what happened to me up there.'

Harry did of course know what had happened to him. The incident nonetheless had left an indelible impression on him. He smiled as he recalled it. Can't follow the big man's footsteps now, he chided himself.

Slowly both the officers got up and gingerly moved in, weapons covering their respective arcs of responsibility.

At their heels was RK, like an impatient dog waiting to be unleashed. The excitement to perhaps find his arch enemy Manzur in the room, injured or alive, was driving him to irrational risks. Harry snapped at him to fall back and had to haul him back by the collar. He didn't know the room clearing drills and would only be a hindrance. Others followed behind and quickly fanned out, with some heading up the decrepit wooden steps. Within a few minutes the 'all clear' was heard from the floor above and Harry switched on his torch.

Someone gave succour to a dying wicker lamp, which was still flickering uncertainly in a niche and carefully, like a couple of detectives, they went over the scene of crime. There was disappointment all around, as no twisted mangled bodies were discovered. The fire in the hearth was still simmering and around it lay an upturned bowl, its content all over the floor, with ash covered rotis scattered across. Harry was worried about the house catching fire and asked one of the men to extinguish the blaze.

'Disrupted their dinner party it seems,' said Shaukeen.

Then RK noticed a blotch of blood on the window sill, but of the militants there was no sign. However, RK was bristling with excitement, like a gun dog latching on to the smell of game and kept muttering it was Manzur for sure who was injured. Harry looked at Shaukeen accusingly.

'What!' said Shaukeen in defence. 'The contact happened so fast, Sir, I didn't have the time to send a bunch across the nullah to put a cordon of sorts. We came to return a bloody goat not to get into a firefight with the residents. This is what happens when you try and be nice to folks. Pity the fucking goat, having started all this, it also seems to have disappeared.'

The contact was reported to the CO and the party began in earnest now. The colonel was a Gurkha and when not wearing his uniform, would often pass off as a young captain. He was a charmer and the officers under him believed that if you could give the colonel five minutes with any mujahid, you wouldn't have to exchange fire with him. But that was not the colonel's style, for his boyish looks were often not in consonance with the aggression he displayed in such circumstances. All knew it would be rock and roll in the mountains for an indefinite period, unless a militant's cadaver wasn't presented to him soon. Sweets were distributed to the village kids the next morning and rewards promised to anyone coming back with info. Everyone considered it a normal contact and the smell of a kill energised the men.

The highlight of the day was when an MI-8 helicopter flew in and to everyone's surprise, out stepped an obese camel-coloured Labrador with his handler. The dog, wagging his tail like a rallying flag, was noticeably glad to escape the rattling flying machine smelling of high octane aviation fuel. Someone in his wisdom higher up the chain of command had thought it prudent to dispatch a dog to track down the wounded mujahid. The biggest chopper had been requisitioned thereafter to deliver the most lethal weapon the Army could think of in assistance to the troops on ground. Harry, while a dog lover, wasn't keen on using them in operations, especially if a firefight was imminent.

The Labradors tested in Sri Lanka were more a burden than an asset and ran out of steam in the muggy weather very quickly. The dogs also abhorred the thorn and fly infested tropical jungle, apart from the strict non-social conduct imposed by the nature of the SF ops, of sitting immobile in ambush for days. Nagaland had been no different, where other than the vicious weather, the jungle terrain was far worse. The dogs tended to collect a lot of leeches. He recalled once in a trans-border op in the northeast of India, the Lab accompanying them, just sat down halfway up a hill and refused to budge. He had to be carried back thereafter. Petting the dog now, Harry directed the handler to find himself quarters in the HQ hut.

'Not required to come up with us,' he told the man. 'Look after the dog and I will spend time with him when I am back.'

CHAPTER 11

Warwan

Men, today we die a little.

—Emil Zatopek

Manzur had one look at the cottage and some of his fears were alleviated. It stood solitary at the edge of the village with a nullah running behind the back garden. Well, he thought, if the rendezvous had to be in a village, then this was the most perfect house to select. He exchanged greetings with the two foreign militants and they settled down in front of the hearth. Apparently they had also just arrived at the house barely thirty minutes ahead of Manzur. The house was not exactly the pre-decided RV—in fact they were in a completely different village, having drifted further down the valley in their attempt to avoid the numerous Army patrols.

A blazing fire spread its warmth and induced a lethargy that invariably follows when creature comforts are suddenly made available, in the aftermath of sustained and hard physical labour.

Manzur studied the bearded gaunt faces in the flickering firelight. One of them was quite tall and well built, while the other, with the bushy beard and a wild look in the eyes, appeared to be the older of the two. He was wearing a black *salwar kameez*, with a *pakul* rammed down his head—the flat wooly Afghan cap, often preferred by the seasoned mujahideen and made popular during the jehad in Afghanistan against the Soviets. It was like an informal badge of honour and in jehadi circles got you the reverence reserved for an experienced man of war. You had to earn it, like the coveted maroon beret worn by the paratroops.

The older man seemed to be the leader. For the tall one showed just that slight reverence, bestowed in this part of the world as an acknowledgement of being more experienced a practitioner in the trade that one follows. Having been in some rough spots together, theirs was an informal ustad–disciple relationship. He was the man who had engaged with Manzur since morning on the radio. The antenna of a small Motorola radio set was sticking out of the pouch of his ammo jacket. But at the moment, the leader and the led were both at the end of their tethers. Manzur had been following the news and the local grapevine on the hostage crisis and knew the men had gone through a lot in the last couple of months. The gamut of the state's security resources were hunting for these men. Their eyes were sunken and they looked completely spent, gazing absently into the fire and dozing off from time to time, as the warmth loosened their fatigued limbs and the fire drew them into its embrace.

Neither one spoke and to Manzur it seemed their minds had shut off, transporting them to a different world. Perhaps they were thinking of their homes far away. He felt it impolite to break into their reverie and decided the conversation could wait till the morning. Before meeting them, he had planned to give them only a short break before taking them back up the mountain. But one look convinced him on the futility of the task. They clearly needed some rest. As per the plan, after the contact was established, Manzur was to accompany them back to Sukhnoi village to meet up with Turki. If he was satisfied with the arrangements, then Manzur was to escort the entire bunch to the place he had selected for them just above Gundoh.

It was a small hamlet called Ghild and consisted of a few Hindu families. The Hindus would of course have to be locked up in one of the houses. Manzur was pleased with the selection, for the village sat atop an isolated hill, at the end of a very steep long climb. The area was commanded by Noora Muhammad, another of those colourful characters that militancy was throwing up from time to time. A J&K police deserter with a black belt in karate, he moved around sporting dark glasses with an Afghan bodyguard in tow. He had an impressive record of having looted a bank, slaughtering a few security men and had the gumption to ambush the local SP nearly bagging him in the bargain. Reluctantly, Manzur had tied up with him for local protection for he had the reputation of being a loose cannon. Some of his own boys were also along to add to the numbers.

To reach the village it would easily take five hours for a large body of men approaching from any direction. His boys and some of the villagers had been given radio sets and would be able to convey well in time, any such gathering of soldiers at the roadhead. Manzur was quite proud to be associated with such a large enterprise, especially one that had gathered so much international attention. This was jehad on a different scale, he had realised. He blessed Malik, who had recommended his name. Inshallah, if things went well and he got the group out, it would raise his prestige amongst not only the local jehadi cadres, but also with the senior commanders across the border.

But all that would have to wait for another day. In the meanwhile, the owner of the house had placed a stack of rotis and a steaming bowl of beans in front of them. Manzur realised how famished he was. The owner, a middle-aged man, telling no one in particular that he was going out to fetch some wood for the fire, promptly walked out. Before any of them could react, he headed straight down the pebble path, which wound its way through the walnut trees to his neighbour's cottage some distance away. He had been to the Army camp earlier that day during the search for his goat and knew how close they were. Then these people had turned up and made themselves quite comfortable in his home. He definitely did not want to be around when the Army came calling.

There is an old saying in Hindustani: 'Every grain carries the name of the man it feeds and every bullet the name of the man it would bleed.' The food lying in front of the trio clearly did not have any of their names written on it, for before the first mouthful could be consumed, the front door suddenly swung on its hinges revealing a goat and two startled bearded soldiers blocking the doorway and gazing at them incredulously. There was a stillness born of surprise as time froze, along with everybody else in and outside the room. Then, with a frenzied motion that comes of fear rather than reflexes, both parties went for their guns and engaged simultaneously. While the two Al Faran militants promptly took position behind the windows on either side of the door to return fire, Manzur had other plans.

Disengaging from the fight, he rushed to the end of the house and got busy prying open a small window in the last room, which had been nailed shut. What a pity, he thought, that local houses had only one entrance in front and no doors behind. He was a local militant, an ex-BSF soldier and knew very well how most of these contacts with the Army ended. And he knew this bunch was of a different mettle—they would trade lead for lead, till either lead or life ran out. He wanted out. Meanwhile the firing outside had picked up and Manzur knew reinforcements had arrived. Now it was a just a matter of time before the Army surrounded the house. They should have made a break earlier when the odds were in their favour. But the Paki mujahids wouldn't hear of running away from the fight. Over the sound of the firing, he heard one of the Paki mujahid desperately shouting for him to cover the left flank. Fear gave him strength and he wrenched at the window.

Using whatever he could get—a rod, a piece of sharp tile—he finally managed to get the window open. Just when he pulled out the last plank covering the opening, a terrific explosion tore through the house, knocking him against the wall. He lay there winded, trying to make sense of what had happened, when another followed. Timber and masonry crashed around him and a thick cloud of dust filled up the room, engulfing him in a dusty embrace. Manzur Ahmad did what most people in his shoes would have done—with arms crossed over his head in protection, he closed his eyes and began reciting prayers that gave him strength, the *kalma*.

He was brought to his senses by the tall mujahid helping along his companion who seemed to be injured. The firing had ceased and Manzur was surprised they were still alive. Quickly they tumbled out through the small opening and in the panic of the moment each man staggered away in a different direction in the darkness. It was clearly each man to himself and only when Manzur had got enough distance between him and the cursed house, having run uphill all the while, did he pause to take stock. Lights could be seen flickering in the house and in the nullah behind, as the soldiers went about the search. It was then he noticed he had carried away the tall man's AK. Strangely he felt relieved he was rid of the two foreign mujahids, for in their current state they weren't going very far and would have also dragged him to an early grave. They had crossed the border, he thought, to attain *shahadat* and they were going to get it now. He, for one, was certainly not going to be a part of the drama when it unfolded.

Casting a quick look below and summoning the last of his reserves, Manzur climbed hard for the next few hours, trying to figure out where he had parted with his companion Aslam. This was the time he needed him most. But in their headless dash for survival in pitch darkness, it would have been sheer luck to have run in the same direction where he had last left Aslam. And luck, for one, was certainly not on his side today. A little later, exhausted and confident that he had put enough distance to be safe from any pursuit, he crashed out under a huge boulder for some rest and daylight.

***

Aslam had sat with his back against a tree, dozing lightly, as he waited for his friend. From his perch, he had seen Manzur enter the cottage almost half an hour ago, and he hadn't emerged with the guest mujahids. Aslam wondered what may be holding him back and should he also slip down to the house for some much needed food and a hot cup of tea. That's exactly what Manzur must be up to, he thought. Aslam must have then fallen asleep, for he was jolted quite suddenly by the rattle of musketry at close range. Gripping his rifle, he slid to the ground, expecting the fire to come his way. Then he realised the target was elsewhere and his attention was drawn below, where a firefight was unfolding with the occupants of the house. It could only be the Army. He stood there rooted to the spot watching, fearful, yet thrilled and fascinated, as more soldiers turned up shortly and the gunfight picked up intensity, escalating shortly into a raging crescendo of AK fire.

Darkness was descending rapidly as he stood there unsure what to do, hoping to catch sight of the besieged men break out of the house any moment and make for the hills. He decided if that happened, he would give covering fire from the top. He could make out the muzzle flash of the soldiers firing into the house. Why weren't Manzur and the others breaking contact and slipping out from behind the house into the nullah, he wondered, for there was no cordon in place yet. Poor Manzur, he thought, it's unfortunate to have got stuck with those crazy Paki mujahids, who must have decided to meet Allah today.

Then, from the direction of the walnut trees, he saw a big flash of light, like a giant spark and in the space of a breath, an enormous explosion tore through the night. Barely had the echoes subsided, that another followed suit, both exploding with such ferocity into the house that, he wondered, if anybody inside survived the hit. As the last echoes died, a deathly silence fell over the place. As his mind and ears cleared, he felt himself trembling with fear at the prospect that he could have also been in the house along with Manzur. Aslam didn't dither long on the spot now. With a silent prayer for his presumed lost friend, he slung his weapon on the shoulder and promptly fast-legged it in the direction of home.

CHAPTER 12

Warwan

With patience first and patience last,
And doggedness all through,
A man can think the wildest thoughts,
And make them all come true.

—George Psychoundakis, *The Cretan Runner*

The contact was reported to the CO who wanted search parties out immediately, but Harry put his foot down. It was too dangerous to track at night, especially when one of the militants was wounded. They would certainly buy unnecessary casualties. At the crack of dawn, as the birds stirred, ruffling themselves awake to alight on the bare fields and before the first rooster in the village had crowed, the dogs of war were slipping out of the posts, with enough supplies to last for the next thirty-six hours. The orders were clear from the CO—the patrol which brings a militant back dead or alive gets a break, the rest can settle down and celebrate Diwali on the heights.

As the sun broke over the crest of the surrounding hills, Harry paused to collect his breath, looking down at the column of men labouring under the loads they carried. He was appalled at the sight, for it looked like an army of porters lugging household goods rather than a fighting patrol. He was reminded of his childhood days in Simla, where it was a common sight to see Nepalese porters carrying goods from the Ring Road up to the Mall. Some of the soldiers had bulging packs which rose above their heads. The buggers were obsessed with carrying load, he thought. In spite of being a member of the tribe, it never ceased to amaze him at the amount of weight some of the men could carry, practically half their own body weight at times. Maybe they should recruit professional high altitude porters in the SF!

The militants carrying just their personal weapon and ammo could run circles around this lot. However, Harry knew that bulk of the weight was extra ammo. Hard experience had taught this lot that when the chips were down, no cavalry was coming to bail them out in a hurry. Well, in a way they were the cavalry for the rest of the Army. In a protracted firefight, one could go without food and water, but you were a dead man minus ammo. Harry also knew the troop would have distributed the load in a manner where the vanguard and the tail would be carrying comparatively lighter loads, to engage effectively in case of a contact.

But what a waste of their specialisation skills. He saw OP and Bajrang coming up the twisting path straining on the steep climb. Both were ace combat free-fallers and had just come back from a demo jump in Delhi. The combat divers referred to them as the glamour boys in jocularity. He suppressed a smile at their state now. Perfect induction to the real SF world.

Behind came a few divers, lugging heavy weights. The only man, thought Harry, who seemed to be absolutely enjoying himself was little Dola Ram. A hillman and a qualified mountaineer who had been an instructor at the High Altitude Warfare School (HAWS), he was climbing effortlessly, taking jibes and digs at the rest of the men.

Harry decided to gain height and establish a commando harbour in the forest, where all the extra weight would be dumped and fighting patrols could be sent out carrying just their weapon and the bare essentials. For the essence of mountain warfare is all about top down fighting.

The healthy rivalry and inherent competitive spirit of the SF now came to the fore, as troops took up the challenge. These were men who considered themselves warriors rather than regular soldiers. The Army was a profession, an adventure for most when they volunteered for the SF and not a career. They firmly believed in the motto 'Who cares who wins' as long as a fight was in the offing and was worth the effort. Adopting the age-old devilish methods followed by guerrillas the world over, of surprise, speed and uncertainty, the SF hunting parties spread across the mountain acreage with alacrity. The options for any man with hostile intent, unfortunate enough to be stuck in the area of search now, dwindled to two—surrender or fight. And as per the unwritten rules of engagement in *Jehad-e-Kashmir*, if you were a foreign militant, then the former option generally didn't apply to you. Not that either party would have wished it any other way. For the Army, it was also scalp-hunting, as every foreign militant killed fetched you Rs 20,000 in cash. Harry desperately needed the funds to buy a TV set for the team.

***

Then luck intervened as it often does, when sheer effort subsumes probability. One of the militants, hopelessly lost and devastated at having spent another miserable night in the open, with no food or water, left the protection of the forest cover and descended to one of the villages. If he hadn't been an unlettered and a desperate man but instead had the privilege of a public school education, one could have ventured to espouse that he was following what Chesterton wrote: 'If you didn't seem to be hiding, nobody hunted you out.' So with great nonchalance, the man arrived at the nearest house and tried to engage with the locals in broken Urdu. If it wasn't for his height, standing well over six feet, and if the local language hadn't been Kashmiri, he may as well have got away, blending easily with the villagers. But Allah had decided otherwise. His course was run and his days of jehad in Kashmir were about to come to an inglorious end.

The morning had gone off peacefully and Harry, sighting a few houses below, instructed Subedar Buta Singh to peel off with a few men and take a detour through the village, before winding up for the day. As Buta approached the first house, he ran into a tall, well-built man standing on the path, looking lost and forlorn, fidgeting about most uncomfortably at the sudden appearance of the patrol. On being accosted, he rambled nervously something about studying in the local school. This reply was very suspicious. Even if he had failed consistently in every class, attaining height instead of grades over the years, he would certainly be older than the average teacher of that school.

Buta smiled, 'And what class would that be? Twenty? Any other excuse and I wouldn't have bothered you, brother. But this answer is an insult to my intellect. Clearly you think I am a monkey's uncle.'

A search of his pockets produced dry fruits, an emergency ration often carried by militants. The villagers around also confirmed he was not a local and could not speak their language. His nervous demeanour, accent and the inconsistent answers were all too suspicious and the man was promptly hauled in for questioning. Havildar Sultan was tasked with the job to loosen his tongue. He was a hard nut to crack and stuck to some cock and bull story which he kept contradicting often. The screws were tightened and just when a decision was taken to introduce him to '*Tanni*, water parade', as it was called by the SF in Sri Lanka or water boarding as the Americans refer to it, the man cracked. He maintained he had no weapon but some other stuff tucked away halfway up the mountain. With his hands tied by a stout rope, he led his captors on a thirty-minute climb from the spot where he had been captured.

From a crevice, in between some entwining overground roots of a large Deodar tree, he pulled out an expensive camera and an electronic diary wrapped in a plastic packet. They were unusual accoutrements for a local man to carry in those parts. It piqued everyone's curiosity—the plot was clearly thickening, mused Harry and would require time to unravel. The prisoner was led back to base and the interrogation resumed with a vengeance. Sultan was busy asking questions as he calmly stuck paper pins under the man's nails. The other innocuous looking tools of interrogation were kept ready in one corner of the spartan room—a bucket of water, a cotton cloth and a field telephone with a 6 Volt battery. To a bystander unaware of the setting,

Sultan's even tone and the prisoner's stoic forbearance to pain could have easily been misconstrued as a normal conversation. But to the man the words were being addressed, the menace in Sultan's voice was palpable and the pain excruciating. Sultan was what they would have called in the old Wild West 'a killing gentleman'.

Harry contributed his two penny bit by twisting the man's ears, like a headmaster dealing with a recalcitrant school boy. The conduct so far had been rather genteel by standards of interrogation, but the mood of the captors was darkening rapidly and the prisoner could gauge that they were getting impatient by the minute. Shaukeen, slumped on some ammo boxes in the corner, was busy fiddling with the electronic diary. Random pressing of buttons suddenly lit up the screen with the word Al Faran in English along with the list of all its twelve members. All hell broke loose now. The prisoner was confronted with the proof, as he looked up dismally at a very pissed bunch of interrogators and realised the game was up. Any further deceit, he knew, was going to fetch him exquisite pain. This was when he started to sing like a canary on cannabis.

The man's name was Shakeel. He was from Gilgit in Pakistan and was one of the core members of Al Faran. Shakeel poured out his tale of misadventure, from the punishment in the mountains as they tried to penetrate the cordon, leading to the contact. He confirmed his buddy, Shoaib Lala, was wounded and in their desperation for flight, everybody got separated in the darkness.

'*Jenab*, a local mujahid leader, Manzur Ahmad, was our guide and was supposed to escort the group to our next safe house.

Unfortunately after the clash, the man disappeared, along with my weapon, or else you wouldn't have got me alive.'

Harry was disappointed that Manzur wasn't the one who was wounded. The man had a cat's life. Shakeel mentioned that their leader Turki killed Ostro, the Norwegian *firangi* as he was the most troublesome and had some rudimentary military training. The entire group, along with the hostages, was holed out further up the valley in a remote hamlet. They were desperate to get out as the location was compromised and under constant air surveillance. Turki feared it was just a matter of time before a rescue attempt was made. All hopes were pinned on the two getting through to Manzur and then escorting the group along with the hostages to their next safe haven.

The wires burned with messages to and fro between the unit and the corp HQ, and a chopper landed sometime in the evening. Without switching off the engines, it barely waited long enough for the solitary broken handcuffed man to be bundled in, before it rose again on its way back to Udhampur. Someone further up the chain of command, with more tools and time on his hand for the task, was going to continue the unpleasant conversation with him. The decision to make a rescue attempt or not, would depend on the intelligence finally milked out of the unfortunate Al Faran militant.

Meanwhile, the remnants of the Al Faran waited in vain with the hostages. The local grapevine quickly conveyed the disastrous message to the group. The two Al Faran brothers were either dead or captured. It was soon clear that movement south was not a possibility anymore and the only bolt hole now lay north. This was big mountain country, where the weather was rapidly turning hostile threatening imminent snow.

Safe havens were getting scarcer by the day. The Al Faran, it seemed, had run their course and were now at the mercy of the weather and the Indian Army. And while the weather might still be forgiving, the Indian Army was not known for that virtue.

CHAPTER 13

Warwan

Gentleman. Gun Fighter.
He never killed a man that did not need killing.

—*Epitaph on the grave of* Clay Allison

Manzur was a survivor who firmly believed that if there were enough good reasons to die in the name of Allah, there were equally compelling reasons to live in his name. For no man ever got anything before his time, or more than his destiny. He would go when his time was up and not before and not after. Training and temperament had further prepared him for such life-threatening situations and the best in him emerged when cornered. He figured that after the contact in the village, the bulk of the troops would now be abandoning the heights to intensify their search in and around the various hamlets strung along the valley.

Manzur decided to gain height and observe the proceedings from his perch. Depending on how the situation panned out, he would take a call—to continue with the given task of escorting Al Faran to safer sanctuaries, or to abort mission. He was a strong man and within three hours of steady climbing, he passed the last of the *dhoak*s now abandoned for the winter and reached the tree line.

Here, his further progress was curtailed and he paused, a worried expression creasing his visage, as he slowly cast a glance upwards. In front rose a veritable wall of grey rocky cliffs, jutting out like the prow of some beached battleship. Bereft of any tree cover, the rocks reached up to the invisible summits somewhere, cloaked as they were now in a thick mist, rolling down the vertical wall like a silent ghost waterfall. Tufts of sturdy brown grass and dwarf Oak clung precariously to the clefts in the cliff, like some desperate rock-climbers clinging for survival. The way ahead was well and truly barred.

He knew that crossing the precipitous mountains in that direction would take days and even if he did manage to emerge at the other end, it would be in a different land, of monks and mongoloid looking people, following a different god than his own. For the barren desert of Ladakh lay on the other side. The only possible exit that he was vaguely aware of was further up through the Kanital pass at over 13,000 feet. In any case that meant going further north into the jaws of death and he was in no physical or mental state to take that kind of risk.

Manzur sat down to regain his breath and plan out his next course of action. Having decided that he was done with all this Al Faran nonsense, he took the decision to head back home via Kishtwar. The thought of home reminded him of Razia and he realised that not once had he recalled her in the last so many hours. Whoever said love is the most powerful emotion and supplants all other feelings, he thought, had clearly never stared death in the face. For in the shadow of death, only life matters. Anyway, he decided to make haste and sort out the marriage issue. He cursed the officer from Bhadarwah who had turned up at the nick of time to complicate matters and now this Al Faran business had nearly put an end to that union. Perhaps the marriage was jinxed and the woman had cursed him.

He smiled at the thought that he had at least managed to right the wrong done to him by torturing that soldier. The bastard havildar was a spy and had led the Army to his whereabouts. The man had confessed as much, though he hadn't parted with the radio set in spite of all the punishment. Then Manzur started to worry if Razia had left the village with her husband, for someone had mentioned seeing her heading down with the Army. He wondered if the soldiers in the Warwan, who were so keen to fix a meeting for him with his maker, may not perhaps be his old acquaintances from back home. The unrelenting perseverance the Army had exhibited in pursuing them, gave him the impression that it may not be all about Al Faran and the hostages and could probably have a personal angle to it. It was a disheartening thought and sent a chill up his spine. He decided to get back home and keep a low profile for some time.

His head reeling with thoughts of sex and death, Manzur had barely taken a few steps homewards, when his radio crackled to life and a plaintive voice came on air appealing for help. The reception was loud and clear and Manzur guessed it was the injured Al Faran mujahid. He recalled Shoaib's voice and remembered that he was the one carrying the radio set. He was also certain that Shoaib was on the same hill somewhere below him.

Manzur was about to acknowledge, when he released the transmit button. It suddenly struck him that the Army may also be monitoring the radio calls. There was no way he was going to make contact. He was not sure how badly the man was wounded, but sending out calls like this, he thought, was tantamount to playing your own requiem. Now his chances had deteriorated further and it was just a matter of time before the Army locked on to his position, if they hadn't done so already. From the anguish in the voice, he knew the person on the other end was badly injured. This led him to the next thought: If Shoaib was injured, where was the other tall mujahid? Why was he not stopping the man from bleating like a goat being led for halal. Was he dead or were they separated? Manzur was in a moral dilemma for he couldn't just abandon a mujahid brother in need. True to his cautious nature, he decided first to scout around discretely without endangering himself. If there was a chance he would help, or else, to each his own fate.

Cautiously he made his way down through the forest, all the time listening to Shoaib's incessant appeals on the radio for help to all and sundry. Different militant stations would lock on from time to time and attempt to figure out his location, promising help. Some offered sympathy, others advice, while one hardened fanatic told him to shut up and prepare himself for the fight. After all, he had come to attain martyrdom and he was fortunate his time had come.

In an hour's descent, Manzur found himself on a little rocky promontory overlooking a hanging valley on his left, while the forested spur he was on ran down at a sharp gradient to the main valley below. He was surprised to have climbed that steep hill so fast, that too at night and in his considerably exhausted state.

Clearly, his fear-addled brain had propelled him up the mountain in self-preservation. Manzur figured he must have climbed for most of the night, before he crashed out under the rock due to sheer exhaustion. He hadn't eaten anything in the last twenty-eight hours and had barely managed a proper shut eye in that time. Since the previous morning, when he had responded to the radio message of the Al Faran militants, he had been up on his feet.

While he couldn't see any signs of habitation, a milky blue chasm at the bottom indicated where the main valley lay and the Warwan river flowed to meet the Chenab. Beyond, the mountains rose again, stupendously, with jagged tops, pock marked with a dash of white, where the snow still nestled in the niches and pockets of the cliffs.

Somewhere on top of those mountains straight ahead, he guessed, lay Margan top, at nearly 12,000 feet, sprinkled with impoverished Gujjar summer settlements, which would now be deserted with the onset of winters. Margan in the local dialect meant Death Valley, a name it had earned because of its unpredictable weather, which very easily turned the place into an windy icy hell. A pony track from Warwan wound its way up and across the flattish meadow, bifurcating on top with one of the branches swinging north to drop on the other side into the Pahalgam valley in Kashmir. All this he had gathered from Irfan, one of his team members, who hailed from a village close to Kishtwar.

In a single thought, he had crossed the Warwan, gone over the precipitous mountains and landed in Pahalgam, a place he had visited once as a child with his father. However, he knew, to reach there in reality from where he stood, would take a hillman three days of stiff walking, starting from the time of azan in the morning till the last call of the muezzin for prayers went out to the faithful. Then his thoughts turned to Aslam and how he had obviously deserted him and found himself getting angry at the man. This was the occasion when he needed him the most and it was the second time he had taken flight from a fight, leaving him alone to face the consequences. Aslam was timid in school, timid now and unreliable in times of a crisis. But then Manzur cooled down instantly, realising that in all probability, he would have done the same in similar circumstances. For Aslam, it couldn't have been a pretty sight from the top, with the rockets slamming into the house and all the small arms fire. It was truly a miracle that they had survived.

The weight of the second weapon was telling on him and Manzur looked around for a possible cache site. He would come back for the weapon later when all the hullabaloo had died down. Selecting a big rock which had a natural niche, he folded the metal butt and slid the AK inside, covering the opening with a small stone. Memorising the terrain features and prominent landmarks, he continued his climb downwards. He passed the Gujjar huts with the doors shut and padlocked heavily, and it amused him to think of the meagre possessions those locks were protecting. For he knew the Gujjars were a stingy lot and other than a few old utensils, the huts would be bereft of anything of value. They could have easily left the doors open.

Crossing a grassy patch, he paused at the edge of the forest, for the ground ahead was carved out in small open patches, falling away in steps. Here the Gujjars had cleared the forest and created their own little vegetable garden. The land, now lying fallow, would be brimming in summers with a hardy crop of maize, potatoes and rough mountain spinach to supplement their diet. Suddenly, a helicopter came clattering up the valley from the south and crossed over. From under the cover of the trees, Manzur watched it go by with concern. It was so close he could see the pilot at the controls and read the numbers on the machine. It dawned upon him that they may be looking for him and his accomplices. He was aware the Army often dropped special troops on the heights from these accursed machines. They could come down using ropes and he now feared the chopper was perhaps picking up the men from the valley below. Something told him to go further would be foolhardy.

He hung around, unsure, wondering where he would run if the chopper suddenly appeared with the soldiers. He tried to figure out which direction it would come from and guessed the best approach would clearly be the hanging valley on his left. Following the contours, it would rise up the valley which was like a giant cone—broad at the bottom and tapering to a point where it joined the saddle above him. In his mind he latched on to a concrete image of the hovering chopper parallel to him, with soldiers slithering out, when a glint from across caught his eye.

He sat down and studied the area. Just 400 yards below and across the valley, at the periphery of the forest, he saw a man. A tiny figure in the trees. A little later a few more tiny figures joined him and Manzur could easily make out they were soldiers and in some sort of a consultation. Their attention seemed to be drawn to something on his side of the valley. One of the soldiers took a lying position and resting his rifle on what looked like a rock, took aim, while the others hung back watching. Manzur knew immediately he was a sniper and his target must be very close to where he was.

Curiosity got the better of him and mustering courage, he cautiously made his way to a vantage point further down. The spot he selected was perfect, for the view unfolding below couldn't have been better. There, a couple of hundred yards or so just below him, in the middle of a cluster of large boulders, he sighted the target of the sniper. Propped against a rock and quite oblivious to his predicament sat a man, unaware that he was at that moment, figuring very prominently in the crosshairs of his killer.

Strangely, it reminded Manzur of the balcony seats for a movie he had gone to see in Jammu once. This was better—it was like being in a huge participatory theatre. The ensemble of actors, he the lone member of the audience, and an unfinished runaway script. For, while it seemed to be the beginning of the end, it had far from ended yet, he thought. The two parties were easily 500 metres apart and the shot was not only top down, but also across a wide nullah with a strong breeze blowing downhill. It was a difficult shot, under any circumstances, unless the name had already been written on the bullet. Manzur was hopeful, for the sniper would get just one shot and if he missed, there was no way they could get their hands on him, for it would certainly jolt Shoaib into some sort of evasive action.

He knew it was Shoaib for sure, from his black salwar—the man he had been hearing on the radio since morning. The way he was sprawled, loose limbed against the rocks, Manzur knew he was injured. Of its severity, he was not sure. But clearly, if he had made it up this high on the mountain on his own steam, it couldn't be that bad. Any suspicion he may have had regarding the identity of the man was removed when he saw the man raise his hand to his mouth. Instantly, Manzur's radio came alive. Briefly he was tempted to shout and warn Shoaib but desisted, knowing it would have the soldiers baying for his blood. He lowered the volume of his radio set and waited, praying the sniper would miss and give Shoaib a chance to make a break. He could then perhaps make a dash and get him out.

***

The lead scout or what the Americans call the point man, stopped at the edge of the narrow hanging valley with steep walls and looked back at Harry for instruction—to carry on climbing or to get across onto the other side. The slopes of the valley were treacherous and it would easily take a stiff two hours of negotiating the slopes to the other side. There were sections where the team would have to rope up to transverse. And with all the effort, thought Harry, there was still no guarantee that the wounded mujahid would be on the other side. Here their movement was concealed with the forest providing enough cover, while in crosssing over, they ran the risk of being sighted in the open patch of the nullah. Or worse, if the militant was anywhere close on the other side and decided to engage them, it would be catastrophic. With no cover, they would be strung out on the rope like clothes on a line, or more appropriately like figure eleven targets at a range. He imagined the scenario, the militant comfortably tucked behind a rock taking pot shots at will and promptly decided against crossing the nullah.

They had been intercepting Shoaib's calls since morning and it had been getting stronger as they climbed higher. Without a direction finder, Harry knew, the chances of finding the man in such a huge forested mountain terrain, was almost impossible. Incredible way the Indian army functioned, ruminated Harry. The bloody Germans were using radio intercepting direction finders during World War II to weed out resistance and underground radio networks, and here they were, in the twenty-first century, still relying on their eyes and luck. It was as if the Army had taken a decision to play fair and be sporting by not introducing any weapon or equipment that gave them an edge over their adversary. They carried the same weapon and gear as the mujahideen, with the sole advantage in their favour that they could throw up overwhelming numbers when necessary and had access to medical care in an emergency.

Throughout the climb, RK walking behind Harry, had kept up an incessant chatter. Harry wondered from where the man was getting the energy to talk, for the climb was quite steep. In spite of not paying too much attention, it struck Harry that RK was trying to get something off his chest. He seemed deeply concerned for the safety of the Hindus in the hills, and more important, some of the folks who were his near and dear ones. A woman was mentioned somewhere in the conversation, but Harry wasn't paying attention. It seemed he greatly feared Manzur Ahmad's tenacity for revenge against him and his family.

'He is a free man, *Jenab*,' he told Harry, 'unlike me. While the SP sahib is kind and allows me some freeway, I can only be a reactive force, invariably turning up after an untoward incident. You know there is bad blood between me and Manzur, and having grown up with him, I know how vindictive he can be. The SP sahib doesn't understand and keeps me shut in that cold cell of his, while my friends and relatives are running helter-skelter to avoid a confrontation with Manzur. Most have fled to Bhadarwah or Jammu leaving their lands and property unattended, while Manzur has the run of the place. How can I protect anyone sitting in a jail? The SP sahib thinks the law of the land will deter Manzur from murderous intent, not realising the man has already gone beyond the pale of law. He keeps promising police action in case Manzur inflicts any further damage to my people or property.'

'What are you worried about?' asked Harry between breaths, trying not to be impolite and showing interest in the conversation. 'Isn't there some sort of a code of conduct between the two of you? Neither party to harm the other's family or property?'

'That code is already down the drain, Sahib,' answered RK dismissively, 'after Manzur killed my father. And you know how effective the local police is in the hills. They have families up in the villages at the mercy of Manzur and his cronies, and in any case, most are from his religion. The other day a bunch of mujahids practically danced in front of the BSF post at Jai and the sister fuckers didn't have the balls to come out and fight them. This kind of weakness emboldens the militants.'

Harry stopped to take a breather. It was turning out to be more like a trek than a military op. The weather was packing up and a thick swirling mist rolled down the heights, assuming grotesque shapes as it curled around trees like a snake. The upper regions of the mountain were already clouded under a white blanket and Harry knew it was only a matter of time before the mist would engulf them completely, rendering the search nigh to impossible, other than adding to the risk of blindly stumbling onto a wounded militant with dire consequences. The mujahid could be anywhere and the strength five reception on the radio was no yardstick to proximity to the source of the signal.

They stood around discussing when RK exclaimed loudly, pointing across the valley. Everybody turned to look and he had to give directions before Harry noticed the dark blob amidst a pile of large boulders. A darker rock, thought Harry. Then the 'darker rock' moved just a trifle. A man for sure. Harry asked for the sniper rifle and resting it on RK's shoulder focused on the spot. The high powered telescopic sight shrank the distance by 4x10 and the man sprang into focus. Long beard, wearing a dark *salwar kameez*, he was sitting propped against a rock, with his weapon next to him. Harry handed over the rifle, his face flushed with excitement. God, he thought! Thirty hours of relentless effort had finally paid dividends. They had found the bastard. But what now!

Sultan, a Jat from the heartland of Haryana was an extremely soft-spoken man, preternaturally calm with an unruffled temperament designed for high pressure. Standing six feet in his socks, his gentle eyes and demeanour often belied the ruthlessness and focus he could summon when the occasion demanded. And the occasion had arrived. A soldier's soldier, he was as steady as the sniper rifle he carried. Sultan was instructed to keep the man in his sights and promptly took a lying position, resting the rifle on his rucksack for support. He asked RK to drop some dry pine needles in the air to gauge the wind current, and the act had to be repeated a few times, before Sultan nodded his head in satisfaction. Then he stuck his cheek to the butt and his eyes to the scope and switched off from the existential world around him.

Harry, watching, realised it was a strong wind blowing down the mountain and in all probability would be a much stronger draft in the middle of the nullah. Briefly he was tempted to counsel Sultan to aim at least an inch up and to the right of the target, but then held back, conscious of the fact that Sultan had more sniping experience than him. The others got into a huddle to discuss the best way to neutralise the man—to cross the valley and go after him, or as someone suggested fire a RL. That's like taking a sledgehammer to a 2-mm nail or more appropriate to the situation, taking a Bofors to a duel, thought Harry. Then another concern added urgency for decisive action. Someone reminded the gathering that Shaukeen was climbing with his boys on the opposite spur and would certainly run into the militant. This was unacceptable to the men—to lose a kill to another troop, especially when they had finally run him to ground.

The sniper, Sultan, was the only one oblivious to the burgeoning excitement around him. He was in what professional sportsmen performing at their peak often refer to as being in the 'zone'. All his senses, heightened to a pitch state, seemed to have coalesced, accentuating the object to be demolished. Impervious to the damp cold earth he was lying on, or the sharp stones pricking through his battle dress, he was still like a tombstone in a graveyard. Mentally shut out from all external distraction, his world had shrunk to the narrow confines of his scope. For all it mattered, you could have played a brass band next to him and he wouldn't have flinched. A quick check of his vitals would have revealed an abnormally slow pulse rate, while his breathing was so shallow that it escaped notice of the naked eye.

The man and his weapon had merged and the sniper, in some inexplicable way, was connected to his target. The only thing that could sever the bond now was the 7.62mm steel-tipped bullet locked in the chamber of his Drugnov sniper rifle waiting to be released. Sultan's prayer had finally been answered. It had taken him seventeen years of hard soldiering and hundreds of rounds at the range to be offered this one shot, and he wasn't going to miss it.

The Old Sniper's Prayer

I've been in the wild, from dawn to dusk, suffering cold and heat,
And all I pray, to the gods of war,
is to let the gun and the game meet.
You have run with the game, often spoilt my aim,
yet never have I cussed your name;
For the hunter and the hunted must meet sometime,
to break the inexplicable chain.
So illuminate the path, where the game runs fast and plenty,
An unwavering resolve, a steady arm and the outcome
I leave to you almighty.
As game exists not for the hunter,
it's the hunter that exists for the game;
And both shall perish in spirit and name,
if the gun and the game don't meet.
I trained mighty hard, in both body and mind,
spending hours on a range,
And all I ask is a shot at last, for all my labour and pain.
A fleeting shadow, a glimpse in the distance, anything to aim;
For how will I ever get a kill, Oh lord,
if the gun and the game don't meet.

Manzur Ahmad was getting restless at the helplessness of the situation. A brother mujahid was about to die and he was doing nothing about it. This was tantamount to being an accessory to murder in a jehadi court of law. More importantly, what would he say when he confronted his maker? While the distance between the two hostile parties was significant, his fear of the sniper rendered him incapacitated to movement, leaving him cowering and reluctant to leave cover. Mustering courage finally, he pressed the button of the radio to transmit a terse warning to Shoaib and then ran down across the open ground to the nearest copse of trees. Two things happened simultaneously. RK, on hearing the voice on the radio, exclaimed loudly it was Manzur. The sniper saw the target jerk his head suddenly and make an attempt to get up. Compensating for the wind drift and the drop, Sultan gently squeezed the trigger, like one would a lemon.

Buffeted by strong winds, the steel-tipped nano piece of lead, travelling at 2700 feet a second, veered from its course just a fraction. It crossed the nullah in the blink of an eye, to catch Shoaib below his armpit with a violent smack. Smashing the rib cage and missing his heart by a hair's breadth, the bullet, losing momentum, seared a damaging path through the internal organs, to exit from the other side, leaving a gaping hole as its signature. The best surgeon in the world, given a chance now, with all the tools in the medical trade available at his disposal, would have struggled to put Shoaib back on his feet. And there was no surgeon coming anyway, only Sultan, who being overcautious, sent another shot chasing. But it was a futile gesture, as the target had already disappeared behind the rocks.

Lying on the ground, Shoaib looked up at the overcast sky visible through the foliage for the last time. He could feel a burning pain, as if someone had inserted a hot needle inside and then the stickiness of the warm blood gushing out, like air escaping a punctured balloon. Rapidly the picture of the branches and the sky overhead became hazy and started to flicker, as he tried to focus in an attempt to keep his eyes open. But the effort was in vain. He was beyond normal thoughts now, with only a fleeting regret as he finally shut his eyes forever to the mortal world, that much against his belief, strangely he couldn't hear the siren call of the seventy-two virgins supposedly waiting for him in paradise.

Manzur was still running when the valley reverberated to the sound of the high velocity shot and then another followed in tandem. He wondered if the second shot was for him. From ten feet away, he had one look at the slumped figure of his ex-charge and realised he was a goner and if he didn't depart the scene soon, he would be one too.

RK was delirious with excitement when he saw a distant figure emerge out of the trees and go dashing down towards the rocks. 'Manzur, Manzur!' he exclaimed, springing up from where he was squatting, as if a snake had suddenly surfaced under his buttock, and urged the sniper to take a shot. Sultan shifted the barrel a trifle and followed the man through the sight, waiting to get a clear shot. But the figure was in constant motion, dashing in and out of trees like a harried Yeti. 'Take the shot, brother, take the shot,' RK pleaded. But Sultan was not to be hurried. His temperament and training was different from the average soldier. He didn't believe in fluke hits—you were either reasonably sure of hitting your target or you didn't engage.

Where he came from, missing your target was a worse crime than not engaging. This was a moving target, darting in and out of the trees in a random fashion, and Sultan got the feeling the man was aware he was in the sights of a sniper and was purposely making it difficult for a shot to be taken.

Watching the going-ons, Harry was reminded of a penalty shoot-out in football, where the goalie has to anticipate the corner the shooter may pick. Harry too urged Sultan to take a shot. If nothing else, at least it would put some fright into the man. But Manzur had already left the scope having disappeared into the forest and the fog, and Sultan lowered the rifle. RK let off a burst from his AK in frustration, but it was way beyond the range of his weapon and Harry ordered him to stop.

Shaukeen came on the line hearing the loud report of the small arms fire.

'Two-five, is that your fire? Heard the sniper. Any luck or you guys zeroing weapons. Hope you are not engaging us from across. Over.'

Harry instructed him to climb along the edge of the spur till he came to a cluster of rocks.

'Be careful. The bugger may still be kicking.'

There was an agonising pause as Shaukeen took in the news. Harry could imagine him feeling pissed at missing a sitting duck which was rightly in his area of search. He must be cursing at not having climbed faster, thought Harry with a wry grin. A grenade explosion preceded his entry to the site. Shoaib was smothered in shrapnel, but it was a grenade too late. For he had long back ceased to exist. Shaukeen reported the man was dead and was the same guy who had been wounded earlier in the contact, for his thigh carried a nasty gash, crudely bandaged with a strip of cloth torn from his kameez. Shaukeen could see that this was about the maximum distance the man could have covered, with the kind of wound he carried and no further. But it was certainly not a killing injury. Some villager must have provided him food, for he was just about to tuck into it, when the bullet put an end to his meal.

He looked down at the dead militant and at the stack of rotis wrapped in a dirty cloth, the knot half open. Bad luck, old boy, thought Shaukeen, two attempts to get a meal and both end in disaster. A while longer and you could have died with a full stomach. Not that it would have made much of a difference. He promptly exchanged his weapon with the dead militant's AK. A fancy weapon with a pistol grip and an attached grenade launcher. Separated by the nullah, the two officers had a brief chat over the radio. While Harry was not in a position to go after Manzur, he was tempted to order Shaukeen on the other side to give chase. But one look at the forested acreage and the impossibility of the task dawned upon him. He gave the order to roll back and with that, both the parties turned and went down for well-earned rest. A few locals that they met on the way down, were dispatched to haul the corpse down to the village.

****

Manzur ran uphill in a zigzag fashion, using the trees as cover, till he reached the Gujjar huts. Pumped with adrenaline, he was gasping like a dying goldfish on a gaff. Halting briefly to regain his breath, he turned south on an unused forest track. For a brief moment he was tempted to climb further to retrieve the cached weapon, but then quickly dropped the idea. Getting out of this hot zone was more important than losing one's life for a bloody AK. The dogs of war had smelt blood and would know no restrain, and they also had the flying machine. Within three hours of stiff walking, Manzur Ahmad finally felt the release of fear, which had completely overwhelmed his mind for so many hours, and for the first time he felt safe since the contact in the house. The danger was finally past and over and he had survived.

Confident that no one could possibly follow him now, or no pursuit was even intended in the first place as he was on the other side of the valley, he paused just long enough to cast a quick glance back, at the savage mountains and the silent gloomy forest around. No different, he thought, to the environment he had grown up in—more remote perhaps, but something about the place gave him the creeps. Maybe it was the intensity of the near-death experience, or the cumulative effect of hunger, sleep deprivation and fatigue playing havoc with his mind. Whatever the reasons, he swore he would never be coming back to the Warwan. Then, with a shrug of resignation at a mission unaccomplished, he descended rapidly to the crossing point on the Chenab across which lay home.

RK was morose on the way back and kept needling Harry to rescind his orders and go back up the hill. He kept insisting that Manzur would now make a break for home and they could cut him off at the river, if they moved fast. But Harry was in no mood to pander to RK's personal vendetta at the expense of his tired men. Their job was to get the Al Faran men and they had. Manzur would have been an icing on the cake, a closure to the old score which was pending—however, it could wait. Harry also knew the chances of cornering a single man in that wide swathe of forested mountain terrain were difficult, if not impossible.

A reception was laid out for the tired men as they rolled into camp. It was a standard practice whenever a team came back from ops. The cookhouse had churned out milk powder gulaab jamuns and halwa, the Indian Army's equivalent of high tea in the field. Served in a sweet shop, the insipid and overly sweet stuff would have had the public hauling down the shutters in no time, but to the sugar and salt depleted bodies, it was the most delicious meal, providing instant energy. There was a general sense of smug satisfaction at getting a hard job done, especially without buying any casualties. For tracking a wounded mujahid was always a dicey job. Harry had once been tasked to track and eliminate a wounded militant in the Lolab valley in Kashmir and the experience had been most stressful and enervating to say the least. Luckily the man had died due to loss of blood by the time they caught up with him.

Chicken was procured locally for the evening meal and rum ration was doled out to the men. Shaukeen couldn't get over his bad luck and was like a brooding vulture throughout the evening, morosely gazing into his drink. Harry tried his best to cheer him up, but knew some of these lost chances would never fade from memory. In softer moments, after a few drinks, with old mates in later life, Shaukeen would remonstrate himsclf for not having climbed faster. Such experiences over time may fade from memory, but they never, never really let go of you.

'Perhaps your grenade got him, so let's just declare this a joint kill,' Harry said, patting him on the back.

Orders were received to continue aggressive patrolling south of Inchan and they were forbidden to cross beyond it, for fear it might spook Al Faran into harming the hostages. 'Just enough show of strength to contain them and gently nudge the lot back over the pass into the Kashmir valley,' were the corp commander's order. Within a day or two the op was called off and the team was ordered to report back. With the emergency over, typical of the Army, they were told no choppers would be available now and vehicles would be waiting for them at Kishtwar.

CHAPTER 14

Pul Doda

Underneath the lantern, down by the barrack gate,
darling I remember how you used to wait.

—Lili Marleen, *Song of the Africa Korps*

While the rest of the team with the CO carried on to Udhampur, Harry with his troop peeled off towards Bhadarwah. In a drowsy state, Harry watched the road as it snaked its way to Doda, hugging the contours of the mountain, with the Chenab flowing below. Originating from somewhere around the Baralacha pass in the Lahaul and Spiti valley, the Chandra Bhaga ran north-westwards and crossing the state of Himachal into J&K became the Chenab. It struck Harry that a river was never pretty per se, but the surroundings made it so. The barren mountains on either side gave an unattractive appeal to the Chenab. The same river flowing through thickly-forested mountains would have been a soul-lifting sight. Certainly not as picturesque as Himachal or Kumaon, he thought.

As a climber, Harry had spent a lot of time in the high mountains and had a great affinity for them and for the hill folks in general. Simple, honest people who lead hard lives.

A moving vehicle invariably induced sleep in him and with the op finally wound up, the body was giving way to the built-up fatigue accumulated over the last few days. He cast a bored eye at the scenery slipping by, conscious that he must stay awake for the sake of the equally tired driver. Any error by the latter would certainly entail a roll down the hill into the raging river below. Just short of Pul Doda, where the Niru river debouches into the Chenab, they peeled south, on the road that follows the former upstream to Bhadarwah.

Halfway to their destination, RK sitting behind Harry in the lead vehicle called for a pee break. They stopped and the men dismounted, some lining up against the mountain to relieve themselves, while others slid down the slope on the opposite side leading to the river below. People stretched themselves and the smokers quietly lit up for a hurried drag. It was when they were getting back into the vehicles fifteen minutes later, that Harry noticed RK was nowhere to be seen. Raising the alarm, he dashed behind the vehicle to check if the weapon was also missing. He was relieved to see it conspicuously placed on the back seat, along with all the paraphernalia of war that RK had been given—additional mags and grenades. There was an excited shout and Harry rushed back to see a soldier pointing at a lone figure climbing a narrow track on the far side of the river.

It was a barren flank of the mountain, with near perpendicular walls where it met the river. A winding path went up the hill and must have been in use probably years ago when they had a basket pulley bridge, the wire of which was still visible across the river. RK must have known this was the narrowest point across the raging torrent. The man was climbing like a possessed horny mountain goat and would soon disappear once he went over a hump of white limestone outcrop, halfway up. Harry grabbed the sniper rifle from Sultan and resting it on the bonnet of the vehicle followed the man's progress.

It was RK for sure and in one hell of a hurry to put some distance between himself and his erstwhile colleagues in arms. Harry was amazed at how the man had managed to cross the fast-flowing Niru and wondered as to how long had he been planning his departure. Sultan standing behind prompted gently that Harry should take the shot.

'Shoot him for what crime?' asked Harry. 'He was a brother in arms once and if he is a murderer then that's for the police to deal with. Let the SP sahib handle it.'

At least the man was decent enough not to have taken the weapon, thought Harry, or perhaps he figured, the weapon was the decisive point—its absence would have certainly earned him a bullet in the back. And he had seen the sniper in action. Harry watched through the scope as RK reached the outcrop. Here, another figure slipped out from behind the rocks and joined him. They seemed to be in conversation briefly and then, holding hands, both of them turned and looked down at the men standing on the road.

Harry took a sharp breath as the figures came into focus. RK's partner was a woman. Her all-black dress, with a red head scarf in sharp contrast, accentuated her femininity. She looked rather petite and fetching viewed from a distance through the telescopic sight. And while the face wasn't very clear,

Harry was certain it was none other than Manzur Ahmad's pretty sister. The last time he had seen her was nearly four months ago, when she had given him a petulant look on parting. Harry smiled, feeling foolish at how he had berated RK for chasing the village skirts and troubling the girl. In hindsight he regretted not having allowed RK to have stayed back in the village, for he would certainly have got the intelligence on Manzur.

Looking up at them, it struck him that there are a few sights in life which leave an everlasting impact and touch a chord somewhere within—a snake writhing on the rocks, an eagle freely soaring in a blue sky, a lofty six over the bowler's head, a right and left in a partridge shoot, a man in the crosshairs of your scope breathing perhaps for the last time, and now, a man with a maiden, silhouetted in the distance on a mountain ridge. By God, thought Harry, what a web of intrigue! How did he manage to send her a message? Was this why Manzur and he were at each other's throat? What a coup de grâce RK had delivered to Manzur and Harry laughed at the thought, wondering if Manzur was even aware his stepsister was RK's woman.

The three reasons for a fight are, as the Afghans say, *zan*, *zar*, *zameen*—women, gold and land. Suddenly it hit Harry why RK had been so garrulous during their climb in the Warwan, rambling about protecting his kith and kin and trying to convey, in an indirect way, the justification for this planned absconding act of his. He recalled now, RK mentioning some woman when they were out climbing in the Warwan, but he hadn't been paying much attention. He wondered what motive could have turned the woman to betray her own family.

Perhaps her Hindu roots from her mother's side or maybe she never could forgive her father for taking a younger Muslim second wife.

The man and the woman stood there briefly, etched against the skyline—a poignant image, and then RK waived, raising a salute in farewell. Harry put the rifle down and waved back. When he looked next through the scope, they had vanished. Harry was amazed at the man's gall to climb a barren hill and then stand there confidently, knowing all along he was in the sights of a sniper. But then, having operated with the team, he knew these men were not wanton killers—they were not like him.

Well, thought Harry, as the curtains finally fall, to kill a bandit sometimes you have to be one. A rogue RK loose in the hills was a better weapon against militancy than a rogue RK rotting behind bars. 'Godspeed RK and may you get Manzur,' he mumbled to himself. Little did Harry know, the inexplicable powers that shape people's destiny were already at work, manoeuvring the different pieces in the jigsaw of life towards a predestined conclusion, like pawns in a game of chess.

CHAPTER 15

Jora Kalan Village

Once more into the fray…
Into the last good fight I'll ever know,
Live and die on this day…
Live and die on this day…

—The Grey (Movie)

RK cast a final look at his erstwhile comrades, standing on the road, their attention locked on him. He could make out Harry leaning against the vehicle, the sniper rifle lying across on the bonnet in front and he felt a pang of remorse at having deserted them in such a deceiving manner. His respect for them had gone up over the months that he had spent with them. They bore all sorts of hardship and privations with the calm fortitude of a fatalist and with an ample dose of gallows humour. These were men who could physically hold their own against the fittest local and they never shied away from a fight.

A rucksack carried each man's needs. Inactivity bored them quickly and their only aim, it seemed to him, was to live from contact to contact. He had seen men from the same fraternity as his instructors in the commando school during the course and if he had been impressed then, he was in complete awe of them now. But there was a method in the madness which RK was not to know. A frugal existence created a sense of impermanence, a detachment with the surroundings, aiding mental mobility and activity. Comfort was an impediment to ops. In fact, given a choice, the men preferred to be in ops rather than back in the unit base, where peacetime military discipline, coupled with constant training only made life more miserable.

However, RK knew, climbing up and down mountains only expended energy and the efforts did not always commensurate in diminishing militant lives. Harry and team were striving hard but the odds were against them. One had to be up in the hills to be in a position to react quickly to real-time intelligence. He also realised that while Harry was keen to eliminate Manzur, his agenda in the game was more broad-based, covering militancy as a whole. His, on the other hand, was a single-minded focus to kill Manzur. While he could fend for himself, he worried about his woman. Manzur was aware of the liaison and had been cool about the relationship with his sister. But that was in the days when they were still friends and the two communities not blighted by this madness sweeping the land. The only reason she was still drawing breath was because Manzur thought the affair was over, with RK being in jail. There was talk in the family to get her married soon. If circumstances had been different, RK would have eloped with her, but not now as a wanted fugitive. The only permanent solution was Manzur Ahmad's early demise.

Time had come to go solo and there was a plan. He knew Manzur would certainly dash to Jora Kalan to meet his lady love first. They had grown up together and he knew Manzur's obsession with women. RK had met the young couple in the SP's office when they had come down from the village with Harry. All he had to do was beat Manzur to the village, lay hidden and bushwhack him at the appropriate place. Manzur had a long walk back from the Warwan and would easily take a couple of days, while he could be in the village by nightfall. Now that the plan was in motion, there was no time to waste and RK, in a state of excitement, dashed about like a man on a mission.

First he deposited the girl back at her house, promising her that he would be back in a few days. He then contacted one of his cousins, Raman Singh, and roped him into the enterprise. While Raman pulled out his father's old shotgun, RK dug out an AK-47 he had cached under a rock next to his house. On one of his clandestine missions for the SP sahib, he had extracted a few weapons from a suspected jehadi supporter he had been sent to eliminate. A shot through the leg had the man bleating about the cache, before RK had put him out of his misery. Handing over a pistol and two AKs, RK had promptly hidden one for himself. 'Good thinking,' he complimented himself again now as he cleaned the weapon and punched the bullets into the magazines.

The cousins then made haste in the direction of Jora Kalan. What took an average villager five hours to cover, they did it in three with RK setting the pace. And before the sun had cast its last rays for the day, they were looking down from the edge of the forest at the twinkling lights coming alive in the village of Jora Kalan. A quick inquiry with the occupants of the nearest house confirmed Manzur hadn't been sighted, and as it was getting dark, they shacked up for the night there. The next morning they went about briefing the residents of the houses on the periphery of the village. RK knew Manzur would come up from Gundoh and would therefore, in all probability, check with the few houses on the eastern side first, before venturing further into the village.

The residents were to tell him that the girl and her husband were hiding in the house of the *fauji*, Havildar Saifullah. RK knew that Saifullah's wife, having lost her husband at the hands of Manzur, would not perhaps make too much of a fracas at the prospect of a gunfight at her house and the retaliations that may follow subsequently. While it was a Muslim village, the community wasn't very fond of Manzur who had been living off their largesse for a long time, other than their disapproval at his forceful ways with a married girl and his killing of Saifullah. None of course knew that RK and his partner were Hindus, for they had presented themselves as mujahideen who had been dispatched by the seniors in the *tanzim* to curb the wayward Manzur.

Saif's wife was a bit reluctant initially but consented when RK told her he intended to kill Manzur. He stuck to the same story about the seniors viewing the killing of a Muslim soldier seriously and that a fatwa had been issued against Manzur. They were here to carry it out. She was then given a choice to go down to Bhadarwah with her kids and seek protection and shelter from the Major sahib who was Saif's commanding officer.

The idea must have appealed to her for she promptly collected her kids, and with a few belongings, silently departed down the track. Manzur now had the run of the place. The worst part in the anatomy of an ambush had begun. The wait.

Manzur, by the time he crossed the Chenab on the second day, had regained much of his old bounce, and the shadow of death which had subsumed his every sense for days, seemed to have receded. For no young man thinks he will die. With every familiar sight, his confidence ascended further like his excitement, which at the prospect of meeting the love of his life, clouded his mind from rational thinking. He decided he was going to marry her right away. Life was too short and patience has its limits. He tried to raise Aslam and some of the other members of the team on his radio, but there was only garbled snatches of conversation and static. He was too far and on the lower side of the mountain or perhaps they had all dispersed back to their villages and switched off their radios, having got wind that the operation had fallen apart. With conflicting thoughts of love and lust, Manzur climbing from Gundoh as RK had predicted, arrived at the nearest cottages of Jora Kalan. Briefly he surveyed the village from the periphery and finding it peaceful, boldly strode forward accosting the first local he saw, cutting wood.

'No Army,' answered the man nodding his head vigorously, 'Aah! Yes the girl with the husband, perhaps at the *fauji's* house. Not sure but that's where I had last seen them go.'

Unbeknownst to Manzur, the man he had accosted was none other than the girl's uncle and while Manzur was invited to sit awhile and have a cup of tea, the man dispatched his young son to warn RK. Raman Singh was just stepping out of the house when the boy ran into him and babbled the news. He dashed back indoors and woke up RK, and within minutes, the two of them had taken position behind an upturned timber bed they had placed in the main room. All local houses followed the same design, where the ground floor was meant for the livestock and the residents had the floors above. The plan was simple—let Manzur walk into the room, and if possible, capture him alive. To give him a slow, excruciating death had become RK's fantasy.

The wait wasn't long and within twenty minutes, through a crack in the window, RK saw Manzur crossing the fields. His rifle slung on the shoulder, the man didn't seem to be suspicious at all, striding confidently on the path through the corn field. RK checked the weapon and tried to go through the scenario of how they would disarm him once Manzur was in the room. He had played the scene a hundred times in his mind since his arrival. And now that the curtains were up, he was getting nervous. It was show time and he exchanged a quick look with Raman, as heavy footsteps sounded on the steps coming up to the first floor. Both of them tensed as a loud knock sounded on the door. It was repeated, a pause...and then the door was pushed a little and a bearded face peeped in.

In a glance, Manzur knew something was amiss and felt the prickle down his spine of imminent danger. He had barely managed to withdraw his face when there was a burst of gunfire. Splinters of wood from the door flew into his face as he turned bleeding and scrambled down the stairs in shock.

RK saw Manzur take a peek and knew instantly the man had smelt something fishy. It was now or never and instinctively he opened fire at point blank range. The face disappeared.

Both RK and Raman Singh rushed out of the room, to see Manzur at the landing, struggling to get the weapon off his shoulder. RK fired from the hip position, but his weapon being on auto mode jumped and the bullets went awry. Even in the SF, where a personal weapon is considered an extension of the body and an inordinate amount of time and ammo is spent training, they don't advocate the hip position. Within seconds, the firing pin clicked on empty and RK releasing the magazine, fumbled to extract the loaded one from his loose salwar pocket. Manzur had reached the bottom of the stairs and was just about to dive into the cattle shed, when Raman Singh knocked RK sideways and emptied both barrels into him. Professionals in the business of violence swear by the efficacy of a shotgun over a rifle in a confined space, for it's like an area weapon. Fired from barely fifteen feet, the Indian ordinance HG cartridges, loaded with buckshot and meant for big game, peppered Manzur Ahmad and knocked him over like a pin.

Manzur's back was riddled with pellets and tiny rivulets of blood oozed out slowly reddening his black kurta. The front on the other hand, when they turned him over, was spotless. Except for wheezing like a chronic asthma patient, the man could have been fast asleep. RK looked down at him quizzically, waiting for him to open his eyes, so that he could gloat over his victory. But Manzur wasn't going to give him that satisfaction. Not now, not ever. Within minutes, the wheezing became a hacking cough and with a dramatic trickle of blood from the corner of his mouth, Manzur Ahmad bid adieu to the mortal world.

'The sister fucker is gone,' RK exclaimed incredulously, kicking the body a couple of times, like one would a stray dog.

He shook his head in disbelief and bad luck. As if Manzur had cheated him of his pleasure and the least courtesy owed to an old friend—to have stayed alive a bit longer. 'Right,' he said, turning to Raman, 'you go down to the Major sahib *jaldi* in Bhadarwah with the news. Jai post is going to get the info soon and guys from BSF will be the first to arrive as they are the nearest. They have done nothing to claim this kill. It rightly belongs to the Major sahib and not even the SP sahib can take credit. I will cut off the BSF guys on the ridge and slow them down.'

Harry was sitting down to a late breakfast of *puri sabji* when an excited bedraggled Raman Singh was ushered into the room.

'So you are saying Manzur is dead and RK wants me to go up to the site and claim the kill. What's the proof? Where's the weapon?'

'Sir, he said the weapon belongs to him for he needs it now. But here's the proof,' answered Raman Singh, handing over a faded card.

It was an old BSF ID card belonging to a Manzur Ahmad with the picture of a clean-shaven young man. Harry turned it over a couple of times and then barked orders to get the vehicles ready. He then turned to Raman Singh.

'You are coming along with us and on the way you can fill me on the story. Must say, that was quick work. Where is RK? His mentor, the SP, is looking for him. Now, if this trip turns out to be a wild goose chase, you are in deep shit, pal.'

They drove up most of the way reaching the end of the road at Jai post by mid afternoon. From there on it was a walk up to Jora Kalan village. The BSF guys at the post warned them it could be a trap, as one of their patrols had been fired upon just a few hours back. There was info about a shoot-out and Manzur's demise and the patrol that had gone out to verify wisely decided to turn back after the firing. Harry nodded and continued. He had been made wise about RK's stalling tactics by Raman Singh on their trip here.

Harry and the team found Manzur's body exactly where he had been shot, at the bottom of the stairs. At first glance, it appeared as if the man was acting, playing possum for a shot, and would spring up on his feet at any moment. Except for a thin stream of blood flowing into a clump of cow-dung, his salwar in front was spotless. The villagers had gathered in numbers and confirmed Raman Singh's tale. Raman had made the effort to cover half his face with a handkerchief, but it wasn't much of a disguise. And some of the locals who had seen him impersonating as a mujahid earlier were rather surprised to see him operating with the army now. The locals, thought Harry, seemed glad to be rid of Manzur. For sure the young couple he had tormented for months would celebrate. They strapped the body on a charpoy and a couple of sturdy lads from the village volunteered to carry it till the roadhead.

High up on a rocky promontory, a lone man stood in the shadows of the forest silently watching the Army column roll down the path. Having stopped the BSF patrol, RK had doubled back to watch the procession carting his old mate on his final journey. A lot of innocent people had gone to their grave before their time in the four years of bloodletting. His life had changed forever. Having tasted freedom, albeit briefly, the thought of going back into a cold cell didn't appeal to him. Now that Manzur was dead, RK believed the SP sahib may not have much use for him and would conveniently lock him up for good. In any case, he was on his last leg and about to retire. The next SP may view his actions in a different light. By the time the last man in the column had disappeared from sight round a bend, RK's mind had been made up. Fate had decided his course, he justified to himself. He was going to live and die a free man.

A two-hour walk and the patrol arrived at the Jai post where the vehicles were parked.

'Right. Mount up and let's head home,' Harry ordered. 'Sultan, ask the radio operator to check with base if the MOH (meat on hooves) has been delivered, for tonight we eat, drink and celebrate. The whole point of hanging around here was the debt that we owed a certain gentleman. And now that the gentleman is filed and receipted, I don't see any reason to be wasting more time in these parts. The valley has more game and that's where we should be heading. Will speak to the CO about it.'

Harry looked out of the vehicle window wistfully at the beautiful forested countryside, on which a thick grey mist was settling down like a blanket. He inhaled the cold crisp mountain air and shivered. And by the time they started down towards Bhadarwah, the season's first snowflakes were dancing earthwards.

'You know what,' he said, turning to Sultan cramped next to him on the seat, 'Manzur may be gone but another man will replace him soon. That's how the wheels of militancy run. I fear we are just seeing the beginning, Sultan, for it will be many years, before the savage hills are tame again.'

Author's Note

Out beyond ideas of wrongdoing and right doing, there is a field.
I'll meet you there. When the soul lies down in that grass,
the world is too full to talk about.

—Rumi

Some wise guy worked out the average life of a militant in Kashmir to be between three to four years and Manzur, by and large came to grief within that time frame. Manzur Ahmad alias Colonel, s/o Shamasdin, r/o Charta village, as per the police FIR No 116/1996 u/s 307 7/27 A, was shot dead in an encounter with an RR battalion on 20/8/96. His close friend turned arch enemy, RK, once out on bail, promptly absconded and positioning himself as the saviour of the minority Hindu population, raised his own gang of armed renegades. Turning to banditry at some stage, he subsequently became a menace in the hills for both the communities. Once Manzur was out of the fray, RK alias Bitta, s/o of Faqir Chand r/o of Batoli Bhaala, knew he was a marked man and sensibly decided to declare his innings and head back to the pavilion.

For he was smart enough to know the age-old adage: 'He who lives by the gun, dies by one' and the gun that would finally dispatch him to his maker, in all probability would belong to the Army. For the local RR unit had started taking an undue interest in him and RK knew hereafter, the clock was ticking and he was existing on borrowed time.

RK would be a middle-aged man now and is apparently languishing in one of the jails that sprang up during the early days of the crisis, in the many towns sprinkled across the Pir Panjals, to cater to the enormous demand for incarceration and apprehensions. However, between the two of them during their wild hey days, Manzur and RK ended up causing a substantial amount of damage to life and property and were the talk of the hills for years. They were childhood friends, the best of buddies and course mates in service, till religion drove a permanent wedge in their relationship, turning them into rivals. The bloody feud lacerated the two communities and widened the chasm of distrust, making reconciliation between the two communities that much more difficult in the end.

Considering the degree of hatred and animosity that existed between them, the machinations to outwit each other and the toil and time the vendetta consumed on both sides, neither of them finally had the grim satisfaction of gunning down the other. It eventually took over a decade before peace prevailed again in the hills, but in that time, no other personality dominated the events, or the psyche of the local people as much as RK and Manzur had done during their time.

As for the Al Faran, it was a one-way ticket the moment they abducted the foreigners. They were pursued and hunted with a vengeance. Turki, along with some of his lieutenants, was killed in south Kashmir subsequently, as mentioned in the preface. The few remaining members promptly dispersed, disappearing into the ever-churning jehadi milieu that existed in Kashmir in those days. For the unfortunate hostages, the end was tragic. The moment they were moved out of the Warwan valley, the trail went cold. Conspiracy theories swirled around thick, like the mountain mist, where they had last been seen.

Some believe they were bumped off by the Al Faran on orders from Pakistan as soon as it was realised that the Indians were not going to capitulate to their demands. Once their usefulness was over, they were a liability to be done away with. Others are of the opinion that a deal was brokered whereby the hostages were handed over to a group of surrendered militants who operated along and under the aegis of the Indian Army. They were then instructed to eliminate the hostages, so as to pin the onus on Pakistan. Whatever the reasons, the plan went awry, with dire consequences for the hostages. They disappeared without a trace. A terse sentence sums it up in the Army file on the subject—'Missing, believed killed'.

BSF deserter takes to looting in Doda

From Fiyaz Pampori

KT NEWS SERVICE

DODA, May 2--An organised gang of armed youth led by a BSF deserter Ram Kumar alias Bittu has become active in Bhaderwah area and its adjoining villages.

The well equipped group is involved in selective killings and lootings in and around Bhaderwah area of land locked Doda district. The group was initially formed to fight against the militants and now was indulging in criminal activities, the sources said.

The gang is carrying out its activities within 25 sq. km. area including Barasu and its adjoining villages. From Pul Doda to Bhalla, across Neeru river and from Bhalessa up to Gandoh. Reports said that about 90 families of both the communities have migrated to the safer places from the area due to the terror created by this gang.

The sources disclosed that Ram Kumar made his presence felt in mid 1994, when he was allegedly released from Bhaderwah jail. He was jailed for his alleged involvement in a criminal case. He was released from the jail on the condition that he will inform the police about the movement of Manzoor Ahmed, another deserter and one time friend of Ram Kumar.

He now is a section commander of Hizbul Mujahideen and joined the outfit in 1994. Ram Kumar did not respond and kept no contact with police. Ram Kumar's group was accorded a good support by the people of minority community when he set afire some houses of the rival group members in the beginning.

(Contd on page 8 Col

BSF deserter takes to looting

(Contd from page 1)

He created a reign of terror in Chakrabati, Batoli and Shiv villages and forced the villagers to flee from the area. The sources disclosed that his associates included – Ajit Singh, Surinder Singh, Rattan Lal and Mohd Ashraf. His three gangsters were killed by the group of Manzoor (HM). Two of his associates in police custody.

It was alleged that the Ram Kumar's group was provided weapons by some local organisations. Some local youth were also motivated by this group to fight against the rival group. The gang looted over a dozen houses in the area and also the weapons including licenced guns from them.

Following the increase in the incidents of looting, villagers have formed a committee and approached the district authorities for the help. The people also approached the Rashtriya Rifles officials for the arrest of these gangsters.

Acknowledgments

I would like to thank Brig Rohit Nautiyal along with CO and officers of 4 RR, for their warm hospitality at Doda and Bhadarwah and for organising my trip around in the hills.

Chauhan, radio call sign—Shaukeen, thanks for narrating the experience in your inimitable style so many years ago. May you always have plenty of meat and drink on your table.

Amazon Customer Reviews

★★★★½ 4.5 out of 5 stars

There is a vacuum in the field of war fiction in India and Abhay's book fills it. —*The Hindu*

The book engrosses you and transports you to the beautiful Lolab Valley in Kashmir ripped apart time and again by violence and bloodshed. —*Mumbai Mirror*

The nerve tingling tale of battles between soldiers and terrorists is interspersed with the narrative of love in all its complex shades. —*The Tribune*

The stunning Lolab Valley of Kashmir.

Cold. Crisp. Serene.

Punctuated by the blood curdling violence that rips apart the stillness of this paradise.

Within the militancy torn valley nestles the ravaged lives of the people who inhabit it. And of the men in uniform who fight for their country.

Set against the backdrop of this rugged milieu is the clash of two charismatic leaders—the inimitable Major Hariharan of the Indian Special Forces, and the volatile battle hardened Pakistani mujahid, Sher Khan. Caught in this bitter conflict is the enigmatic Sahira, a local Gujjar girl who has to face her own demons. All of them have journeys that will test their strengths over and over again…

In the Valley of Shadows is a compelling tale of courage and passion and the hatred that an insurgency generates, leaving a trail of destruction and devastation in its wake. Follow the thrilling cat-and-mouse game between two passionate men of war, a chase that only one of them will survive…

In the Valley of Shadows • Abhay Narayan Sapru

ISBN: 978-81-8328-184-3 • ₹295

Amazon Customer Reviews

★★★★½ 4.6 out of 5 stars

This riveting tale of rivalry between an Indian Special Forces officer and a battle-hardened LTTE commander based on realistic settings comes as a breath of fresh air in a market where war books are few and far between.

An action-packed and fast-paced read. ***—Business Standard***

The Beckoning Isle is the story of the degeneration of a society and the vicious politics of retribution. But it is also a tale of two men, on opposite sides of the battle, united only by the fatalism of their ideologies. Abhay Sapru offers a unique perspective of the Sri Lankan War in an engaging, page-turning account of the clash between the Indian Peace Keeping Force and the LTTE, with voices from both sides of what will go down as one of history's great tragedies. **—Shashi Tharoor**

The dense impenetrable jungles of north-east Sri Lanka.

Hot, dank and given to unleashing unsuspecting savage violence.

Inhabited by wildlife and home to a new species—the Tamil Tigers. To hunt the latter, in pursuit roam a band of hard fighting men from the Indian Special Forces.

The Beckoning Isle is a powerful tale of two men of war—the young and devoted Captain Hariharan of the Indian Special Forces and the thinking battle-hardened LTTE commander Silvam. Their destinies are inextricably linked, as their paths often cross from India to Sri Lanka, hurling them each time towards a bloody confrontation. A web of enigmatic politics, raw human emotions and unflinching faith in one's cause make this book unputdownable.

The Beckoning Isle • Abhay Narayan Sapru
ISBN: 978-81-8328-491-2 • ₹295